HER SHELTER

TERRI ANNE BROWNING

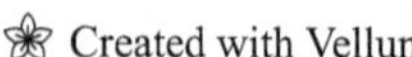 Created with Vellum

PROLOGUE
DELANEY

Hunger twisted in my stomach, gnawing on my insides, making it hard to focus on anything but the empty feeling. I couldn't remember the last time I'd had a full meal, just a vague memory of a small serving from the soup kitchen in Oakland.

I hadn't gotten to finish it because I'd thought I'd seen one of Uncle Tony's men outside the shelter, and I knew I couldn't chance being found.

My uncle wasn't a good person. There was a reason my parents had never talked about my dad's sister and her husband. But when they died, I had no choice but to go live with them. When the social worker dropped me off, sticking around to make sure I settled in, Aunt June and Uncle Tony had been so nice and welcoming.

The moment she left, however, things had changed drastically.

I shuddered, not just from the chilly spring night air on my bare arms, but from the memories of having spent the last eight years under the same roof with those two evil monsters.

I was ten when my parents died. We'd been on vacation in Belize when a gas line had exploded.

Our hotel was right on the water, only a quarter of a mile from the gas line. Dad and Mom were standing on the balcony of our hotel room enjoying cups of coffee when the line blew up. I'd just walked out onto the balcony, already begging them to take me down to the beach.

Dad saw what happened and jumped up, scaring me more than the sudden loud noise. There wasn't time to react, but he'd tried so hard. He pushed Mom and me into the hotel room, using his own body to protect us from the blast.

I was knocked unconscious from the force of the explosion and didn't wake up for nearly a week. When I opened my eyes, it was to discover I was not only an orphan, but also completely deaf.

By the time Aunt June was tracked down and I arrived at her house, I knew some sign language to help me communicate, but I mostly got by with reading lips. My aunt and uncle treated me like I was an idiot, and I was placed in a school for the disabled. Most of the kids in my classes were just as deaf as I was, but the majority of them had been born not being able to hear.

The silence I was suddenly enveloped in every moment of the day made me feel alone in the world, even when I was surrounded by people. Aunt June and her husband didn't even attempt to learn sign language to try to communicate with me. When I wasn't at school, they kept me in my room. Their housekeeper brought me meals and washed my clothes, but other than that, I had no human contact with anyone if I wasn't at school.

Then, the day before my eighteenth birthday, Marta, the housekeeper, appeared in my room with a bag in one hand

and fear in her eyes. She grabbed my face and spoke slowly, knowing I could read lips.

"You have to run, *mija*," she'd mouthed. "It's not safe for you here."

"Why?" I'd asked, confused.

"They are bad people." The urgency I'd felt vibrating off her only made me anxious. "Please, Delaney. You must go. You're not safe."

"But..." I'd started to argue, but she'd pushed the bag into my arms.

"I gave you some money and food. There are clothes and things you will need. Run, *mija*. Run, run, run. Please." She wrapped her arms around me, and I felt her tears on my neck. When she pulled back, her eyes were already swollen. "Run and don't ever let them catch you."

I didn't understand why she was making me run, but I knew she was right. Aunt June and Uncle Tony were evil people. From my bedroom window that overlooked the driveway, I'd seen some of the men who came and went. I'd also seen the women they brought with them.

I ran, and I kept running. From one town to the next, keeping my head down, living in shelters and eating at soup kitchens when my money ran out. Something that happened all too quickly because Marta hadn't given me much cash. In my heart, I knew she'd given me what she could, but it hadn't been enough to last even a week.

From Oakland, I'd hitchhiked north. The trucker who'd dropped me off the day before had stopped in some little town called Creswell Springs, and while he'd been in the gas station just off the interstate, I'd made a run for it. The guy had given me a bad feeling, and after having been on the streets for the past two months, I'd learned quickly to pay attention to that particular feeling.

That was two days ago, and I'd been sleeping in the woods during the day and exploring the small, quaint little town at night. There wasn't much to it, but it seemed safe enough.

My stomach clenched painfully as I walked past a building with a sign that read Ink Shoppe on the window. The lights were off, but a motorcycle and a small white car were in the back parking lot. I'd noticed there were a lot of motorcycles in Creswell Springs. Every man who rode one had a vest that said Angel's Halo MC on the back, but for some reason, they didn't scare me. Not like the men in suits who came to Uncle Tony's house did.

As I rounded the corner of the Ink Shoppe, the back door opened, and I quickly stepped into the shadows. A tall guy with short dark-brown hair stepped outside and opened one of the trash cans. After depositing the bag in his hands, he placed the lid back on it and walked back inside.

I'd seen the outline of a pizza box in that trash bag, and tears filled my eyes as my stomach cramped yet again.

No, I told myself as I turned to walk away. That was gross. Eating food that had been put in the trash was disgusting. I couldn't. I wouldn't.

I walked farther down the road, sticking to the shadows so no one could see me. But no matter how hard I tried to think about anything else, all I could see was the trash bag and the possible pizza box inside. Was there any left? Could there be a piece still, or even some crust? Were there other things in that bag I might be able to eat?

I just needed a little food. Something, anything, to make the pain in my stomach go away.

Pressing a fist to my mouth, I bit down on my knuckle, hoping the pain in my flesh would distract me from the crazy thoughts in my head—and the pain inside me.

An hour passed, and suddenly I was running back to the Ink Shoppe. The discomfort was just too much to take anymore. I was starting to feel dizzy, and I knew if I didn't eat something soon, I was going to be too weak and sick.

When I reached the shop, the motorcycle and the car were still in the parking lot, but all the lights were off inside. The smell of the trash from the other can was rancid, but that didn't stop me from tearing the lid off the one I'd seen the guy open earlier.

In my rush to get to what was inside, the trash can tipped over, crashing to the ground at my feet. Scared, I looked around frantically, unsure how loud the noise had been, but I'd felt a small vibration in my feet, so I knew there had to have been enough ruckus to alert someone to my presence.

Shaking from hunger and fear of being discovered, I quickly tore open the trash bag and pulled out the pizza box. There was also a foil container that smelled like it might have held pasta, and I grabbed that as well. Holding on to them like a lifeline, I took off at a dead run back into the woods.

When I was a good distance away, making sure the shop was out of sight, I stopped and fell to my knees, unable to go another inch because I no longer had the energy.

My sobs made my chest vibrate as I opened the pizza box in the dark and felt around inside for something to eat.

When my fingers touched a small piece of crust, I closed my eyes and stuffed it into my mouth, trying not to think about the fact that I was eating trash. As I chewed, I felt for more, hoping there would be something else. There was half a piece, and from the feel of it, most of the toppings were missing. It was basically just bread and a little sauce, but it tasted so good, it brought tears to my eyes.

Dropping onto my bottom, I pulled the box into my lap, but it was empty now. Placing it on the ground beside me, I reached for the foil container. With the trees blocking out all light, I couldn't see what, if anything, was inside, so I just stuck my hand into it. The spaghetti felt slimy, but when I lifted a handful to my mouth, it tasted good.

As with the pizza box, there wasn't much inside, but it was enough to make the pain in my stomach ease a little. But as I swallowed the last bite, I felt sick.

I'd just eaten trash.

Disgusted with myself, I pulled my knees up to my chest and pressed my forehead to my thighs as I willed the contents in my stomach to remain there. After a few minutes, the sick feeling eased, but I stayed where I was.

The loneliness I'd felt since waking up to complete silence all those years ago pressed down on me, making my heart ache. I missed my mom and dad. I even missed Marta. She didn't have a lot of contact with me, but she'd been the only one to care for me over the past eight years.

Now, I was homeless and starving. There was no one to care if I was hungry or warm or safe.

There was only me, and I was doing a craptastic job of taking care of myself.

I sat there and cried until there were no tears left, but that could have just as easily been because I was dehydrated.

Forcing myself to stand, I brushed the dirt off my clothes and walked farther into the woods to find somewhere to sleep for the night.

1

DELANEY

THE FOG FELT EERIE, BUT I WASN'T SCARED OF THE DARK ANY longer. Over the past two weeks, I'd gotten used to it, even welcomed it at times. Thankfully, it wasn't cold and the rain had stopped, so I didn't have to worry about finding somewhere to keep dry.

The first time it rained, I'd been able to find shelter in the Ink Shoppe after discovering one of the windows was left unlocked. I'd snapped my fingernail back getting the window open, but it had been worth it when I found the blanket in the storage room and was able to cover up after being so cold for so long.

After that, I'd gone back once the tattoo parlor closed each night. At least until they had discovered what I was doing. I suspected it was the girl who worked there, because she'd left me the blanket along with some bottles of water and snacks. I'd been thankful for all that she'd given me, including the few nights of restful sleep within the safe walls of the shop, without calling the cops on me.

But the blanket didn't fare well under the rain that came over those next few nights, and I'd attempted to find other places to bunk down. But those places didn't feel as safe as the Ink Shoppe had. Not to mention, the business owners had called the cops. When I would chance going back to those places, a cop car would be out front, watching the place.

I'd had no choice but to move deeper into the woods or risk being discovered. Now that I was eighteen, I didn't know if the cops would arrest me or send me back to my aunt and uncle. Being arrested didn't sound so bad, but I couldn't chance that they would send me back to Uncle Tony.

My stomach growled angrily as I crept through the shadows toward Aggie's, the restaurant I'd discovered after eating what was left in a takeout bag the girl from the Ink Shoppe had tossed in the trash one night. After reading the name on the bag, I'd walked around Creswell Springs one night in search of the establishment that had amazing hamburgers, even when they were ice-cold.

Their trash always had something salvageable for me to eat, but I only went every other night because I didn't want to risk getting caught. The last time I'd gone, I'd even gotten a tiny slice of chocolate cake, and I was hoping for something sweet to go with my dinner again.

The fog was thicker in places, making it almost impossible to see unless I was directly under one of the streetlights, so I didn't see the headlight of the motorcycle until it was almost too late. Jumping out of the way, I watched as the man driving the powerful bike veered sharply to avoid hitting me. It turned over, landing on his leg as he and the bike slid several yards before coming to a stop with the help of a tree.

Heart pounding, I just stood there, frozen with terror that I'd just caused someone's death.

After what felt like an eternity, the guy slowly lifted up onto his elbows. Shaking his helmet-covered head as if to clear it, he stood. As he got to his feet, my eyes widened at how tall he was and how easy it was for him to lift the heavy piece of machinery off himself in the process. As he did, the fog began to clear, making it easier to see him with the streetlights shining only a few feet away.

He was wearing dark-washed jeans, a white T-shirt, and one of those Angel's Halo MC leather vests the majority of motorcycle riders in this town always wore. As he took off his helmet, I noticed that his jet-black hair was cut short and his facial features were…masculine, yet so beautiful, I couldn't look away from him. When he glared in my direction, there was no mistaking his eyes were my favorite color of metallic blue.

The color entranced me, hypnotizing me into taking a step in his direction.

Before my eyes, his glare changed into a frown, and then he lifted a hand to rub at his chest. When he took a step toward me, he stumbled. Realizing he was hurt, and that I was the cause, I felt my heart constrict while tears stung my eyes.

But then he righted himself. His lips moved, but I was too far away to read the words. His steps increased, and I could tell he was getting angry with me again. Scared that he was going to call the cops and have me arrested, I turned and fled.

Even in the dark, with the fog still lingering in spots, I ran easily through the woods. This had become my home, and I knew it well. There were probably places only I knew where to hide.

But his legs were longer and much faster than my own. I'd barely run a few yards before his strong arms grabbed me from behind. He jerked me around to face him, his lips moving too quickly for me to read what he was saying.

"…hurt…" was the only word I got, and my tears spilled over my lashes.

He was hurt, and it was all my fault.

I lifted my hands, signing that I was sorry, that I didn't mean to make him wreck, that I would find him help.

His brows pulled together, and he gazed down at me for a long moment with an odd look on his face before he caught my hands. Lifting my left one, he examined my finger with the missing fingernail.

After I'd snapped it trying to get into the Ink Shoppe that first night, it had started to get infected. It had swollen and turned red until the rest of the nail had been pushed from the roots. It had hurt so badly, and I'd tried to keep it clean, but it was still painful and warm to the touch.

I balled my hand into a fist so he couldn't see the wound. It was ugly and dirty, just like the rest of me. I couldn't remember the last time I'd had a shower, and I knew I probably smelled just as rancid as the garbage I picked through at night, but I'd grown nose-blind to my own stench weeks ago.

His hands were so much larger than my own, one of his easily enveloping both of mine like it was nothing. Lifting his other hand, he surprised me when he signed, "I'm Max," while speaking the words.

My heart stopped when I realized he could sign. No one outside of school had ever signed with me in the eight years I'd been deaf. My tears fell faster, and I held my breath as he released my hands so he could use both of his own to sign again. "I won't hurt you, little one. Don't be scared."

Blinking back the moisture from my eyes, I gave a nod. For some reason, I believed him when he said he wouldn't hurt me. Maybe I shouldn't, because he was a stranger, but he was the first person I'd been able to communicate with in months.

Max reached out and stroked his thumb over my cheek, wiping away one of the tears that had spilled over my lashes.

Turning his hand over, he looked down at it with a frown, and my face filled with embarrassed heat. I was filthy, and he was probably disgusted from the mere sight of me.

"What's your name?" he signed.

I could have lied, but I wanted him to know my name. "Delaney."

"What are you doing out here all by yourself?" he demanded, his hands moving quickly, while his mouth twisted in anger again. "You could have gotten yourself killed walking out into the road in this fog."

I lowered my lashes, not answering. I didn't want to tell him I'd been on my way to Aggie's to find something to eat in the restaurant's dumpsters.

He lifted my chin with his forefinger, making me look at him again, his face softening. "It's okay, little one," he signed, his lips moving slowly. "Let me get you home."

Frantically, I shook my head, quickly signing that I couldn't go home. To please, please not make me go home.

"Okay." His arms went around me, pulling me against him. He held me for a few moments, and some of my fear of having to face Uncle Tony eased. But all too soon, he was stepping back. "I won't make you go home, but you can't stay out here. Come with me."

He held out his hand, and I didn't even hesitate to place mine in his. His hold was firm yet gentle as we walked back to his motorcycle. When we reached it, he seemed reluctant to release me, but after a brief hesitation, he let go. Pulling his phone from his pocket, he turned on the flashlight so he could examine the damage caused by the crash.

Once he was satisfied it was drivable, he got on and started it up, then offered me the helmet he'd been wearing earlier. I took it, but my fingers fumbled with the clasp.

Pushing my hands aside, he fastened it himself before helping me onto the back of the bike.

Instinctively, I wrapped my arms around his waist and pressed my face into his back. I felt his chest vibrate and loosened my hold, worried I'd caused him more pain. He hadn't limped any on the walk back to his motorcycle, but that didn't mean other places hadn't been harmed during the wreck.

His hands wrapped around my wrists, pulling my arms tighter around his middle once more. I felt his thumb caress over the backs of my hands, and then he squeezed them, as if telling me to hold on tight.

I'd never been on the back of a motorcycle before. It was kind of exciting and a little scary, but oddly, I felt safe with Max in control of the beast-like machine beneath us.

When he pulled into the parking lot of the local mechanic, I was a little sad that the trip was over so quickly. The vibrations of the bike stopped, and then he was offering me his hand to assist me off.

"I have an apartment above the shop," he signed, and I turned to look back at the garage.

The place was huge, with multiple closed garage bays. The storefront was dark, but the place was well cared for. There were no lights on above the shop, no way of telling me how big the apartment might be.

With his hand at the small of my back, Max guided me around to the side of the garage and up the flight of stairs to the second floor. After unlocking the door, he reached in to flip on a light and then urged me forward. Cautiously, I stepped over the threshold, my eyes taking in everything all at once.

A leather couch was against one wall, a simple coffee table between it and the large TV stand that held a giant television set. Pictures decorated the walls, and I spent a moment examining them as I took a few more steps into the apartment.

Some were of Max with a girl who was drop-dead gorgeous. At a glance, I knew she must be his sister, with their matching metallic-blue eyes, dark hair, and impish grins. There were two of Max holding an adorable little boy, and for a moment, I thought maybe it was his son. Until I saw a picture of the girl holding the baby lovingly while a man covered in tattoos tucked them both against him. The pure love and adoration that glazed the inked man's eyes told me this was his family.

Others caught my attention. There were more pictures of Max with an older blond woman than there were with the girl I was assuming was his sister. In all of them, Max had his arm around the blond woman, and that impish grin was even more pronounced.

Max touched my arm, pulling my gaze to him. "That's my mom," he signed. "Raven." He pointed to the ones with the girl, baby, and inked man. "This is Lexa, my older sister. Her son, Finn, and her husband, Ben."

"Finn looks like you," I signed back, and he grinned.

"Yeah, and Ben hates it." He gently caught hold of my wrist and tugged me toward the kitchen. Flipping on the light, he guided me over to the small island and pulled out one of the two stools. Lifting me like I weighed no more than a feather, he placed me on the seat before crossing to the fridge and pulling out containers of food.

I felt my stomach growl, and he snapped his head around with a frown. Embarrassed, I lowered my gaze to the island until he placed the containers on the counter in front of me. Tipping up my chin, he skimmed his thumb over my bottom lip for a moment.

I held my breath as his metallic eyes lowered to my mouth for the longest time, causing my heart to pound almost painfully against my rib cage. Max had to be the most beautiful guy I'd ever seen in my life—and I had the crazy idea that maybe he wanted to kiss me.

But he quickly dropped his hand and straightened. "My mom keeps my fridge stocked. I've got lasagna, chili, pot roast, and meatloaf," he signed with an easy smile. "What do you feel like eating, little one?"

I glanced down at all the offered food and felt my stomach growl again, this time painfully. Wrapping my arms around my middle in hopes of easing the ache, I licked my lips. It all looked so delicious, and I couldn't decide which one I wanted more.

When he touched my chin again, I closed my eyes, savoring the touch. When was the last time someone had touched me?

Marta hugging me before making me run away filled my head, and I had to swallow the sudden lump that clogged my throat.

Max stroked the backs of his fingers over my cheek, encouraging me to open my eyes. "You can have it all," he assured me. "Whatever you want, just say the word."

My teeth sank into my bottom lip to keep it from trembling. It took a few moments before I could get my emotions under control. "Can I…take a shower?"

2

MAX

I stood in front of the microwave, trying not to think about the ethereal angel currently naked beneath the spray of my shower.

A part of me wondered if this was all just some dream. That maybe I was in a coma after wiping out on my bike earlier. My mom was probably standing over my hospital bed. Tubes would be coming from various parts of my body, while wires connected to machines told her I was still alive. No doubt she would have that stoic, emotionless look on her face so she could stay strong for my dad. While deep inside, she would be an emotional wreck because her baby boy was clinging to life by a thread.

But the pain along the entire right side of my body told me that this wasn't a dream and that I was very much awake. I hadn't examined the damage yet, but I could feel the road rash on my leg and side. Nothing seemed broken, but my ribs were no doubt bruised all to hell, and my knee was throbbing.

Yet while Delaney had been right in front of me, I hadn't felt so much as a twinge of discomfort. My focus had been solely on taking care of her, making sure that she was unhurt, that she wasn't frightened of me.

From the looks of her, I could tell she'd been living on the streets for a while. The sheer terror on her face when I first met her pretty brown gaze told me she was running from something—or someone.

She was dirty, hungry, and all alone.

But I would make sure she didn't have to worry about anything ever again.

The lasagna finished heating, and I replaced it with the pot roast. With the way her eyes had lingered on both of their containers, I knew she would enjoy those the most. I reheated both of them first so they would be ready and waiting for her once she was finished showering.

Closing the microwave door, I punched in the time Mom had said to set it for and then rubbed my hand over my chest again. I felt a pressure that had been there since I first set eyes on Delaney earlier. It wasn't painful, or even uncomfortable, but the feeling was something I was unused to. When she was close enough that I could touch her, the pressure eased some-what, but when I didn't have my eyes on her, it intensified.

I wasn't sure if I should be worried about it. Mom would be able to tell me if I should go to the ER or not, get Doc to check me over. But I didn't want her to know I'd wiped out on my way home.

And for the moment, I didn't want her to know about Delaney. Selfishly, I wanted to keep her all to myself for a while. Get her to trust me. Let me take care of her.

That feeling was somewhat alien as well. Other than a few select people, I'd never wanted to take care of anyone besides myself. I'd only known Delaney for less than an hour, and she was already twisting me inside out.

By the time the microwave alerted me that the last container was reheated, I'd plated everything else, as well as pulled out the cake Aunt Flick had made for me and dropped off the day before. It was my favorite—lemon, with a lemon custard in the middle and a lemon cream cheese frosting. Between her and Mom, I never had to worry about cooking for myself. But if I had any hope of keeping Delaney around, I needed to figure out how to feed her without either of them suspecting I had a houseguest.

At least for the moment.

From the bathroom, I heard the water turn off and bit back a groan as I pictured my little treasure rubbing my towel over her sweet little body. She would smell like me since I didn't have any girlie shampoo or body wash. That thought had my cock turning to steel in my jeans, and I quickly adjusted myself.

I'd left her some sweats and a T-shirt to change into. Tomorrow after work, I planned on getting her some new clothes and personal items. But I liked her being in my clothes a hell of a lot, so I wasn't in a hurry.

Grabbing us bottles of water, I set the drinks by our plates and waited for Delaney to join me. When she walked out of the bathroom with her long, damp hair falling over her shoulders and my clothes hanging off her, I nearly swallowed my tongue.

Covered in dirt and grime, the girl had been so hauntingly beautiful I was sure she was an angel sent from above to take me to heaven. Freshly showered, her brown eyes no longer filled with fear, she stole the air from my lungs. Her skin had a natural sun-kissed tone to it, her dark hair dropping almost to her waist. She had the prettiest little nose that slightly turned up at the end, and her lips…

Fuck, those lips.

I wanted to taste them, see them wrapped around my cock…

No, I mentally snarled at myself. I was not going to treat my sweet little treasure like one of the sheep at the clubhouse. She was too precious. I had to take my time and earn her trust…and hopefully more.

Shyly, she stood in the kitchen doorway, her cheeks a rosy pink from the heat of the shower. I forced down the urge to grab her and fuck her against the nearest wall. Giving her a smile I hoped set her at ease, I motioned for her to join me at the island.

"Let's eat, little one," I said aloud as I signed to her. I'd never been so happy that Mom had taught me ASL. I'd taken it as my required language class in both middle and high school too. My dyslexia had put me off trying to learn Spanish or French, and American Sign Language was something Mom had pushed to be taught in our local school system.

Delaney sat down beside me and slowly picked up her fork. Her movements were measured, as if she were forcing herself to hold back and not devour the food set before her, like she was starving. The thought of her hungry made my hands clench at my sides. Growing up, I had never had a lack of food in my life, but I knew that wasn't the case for other kids. Knowing my little treasure had gone without caused me physical pain.

The pressure on my chest doubled until I lifted my hand and carefully pushed her hair back from her face so I could see her better. "There's plenty more where this came from. Eat whatever you want."

She licked her lips as she watched my hands, and then she nodded. She took a small bite of the pot roast first. As her lips wrapped around her fork, her eyes closed and a moan slipped from her. The sound was so innocent, yet so fucking erotic, I had to grip the side of the island to keep from reaching for her.

Her eyes snapped open, and she blushed, mouthing, "Sorry," before taking another bite, this time with some of the baby potatoes and carrots.

Groaning, I turned my attention to my own plate. I'd gone for the meatloaf, leaving the chili in case Delaney was still hungry after she finished her lasagna and pot roast. Given how tiny she was, I wanted to feed her until she begged me to stop…

And then I wanted to feast on her.

Holding back yet another groan, I ate in silence for a while, watching her out of the corner of my eye. Each bite she took was delicate, almost artful. I enjoyed watching her more than I did eating—and considering Mom's meatloaf was one of my favorite things in the world, that was saying a hell of a lot.

After only a few minutes, she set down her fork and then wrapped her arms around herself, a pitiful sound leaving her throat. Her face turned red when she noticed me watching her with concern, and her chin began to tremble again.

Instead of asking her what was wrong, I uncapped her bottle of water and offered it to her. Hand trembling, she took it from me and sipped from it. After a while, she began to relax again, and I figured her stomach pains had passed. Without looking at me, she picked up her fork and thankfully began to eat once again.

When her gaze fell on my plate, I lifted a bite of the meatloaf and mashed potatoes to her lips. Without hesitation, she opened her mouth and accepted the bite. I was rewarded with that little pleased moan, and I couldn't help grinning.

"My mom makes the best meatloaf in the world," I signed as I spoke. "It's my favorite."

Her eyes brightened. "My mom made the best enchiladas. It's one of a million things I miss the most about her."

"She's gone?"

Delaney gave a tiny nod. "She and my dad died in an explosion. When I lost my hearing." She shuddered, and I was quick to wrap an arm around her shoulders in case she was cold. "I was sent to live with my dad's sister and her husband when I was ten."

"I'm sorry you lost them." I tucked a few strands of hair behind her ear, wishing I could offer more comfort than just words, but suddenly, I needed to know how old she was. At first glance, I thought maybe she was at least twenty, but the longer I looked at her, the younger she seemed. "How long did you live with your aunt and uncle?"

"Eight years. I left..." Her hands paused before continuing. "I left the night before I turned eighteen. That was about ten weeks ago."

Relief washed over me that she was legal. Not that I was all that confident I would have been able to keep my hands to myself if she weren't. This little treasure was filling me with emotions I didn't even have a name for, but I knew I would kill anyone who tried to take her away from me.

When Ben and Lexa started dating, I'd scoffed when my sister told me their love had been instant. One look and she knew she wanted to be with him. That he was the sheriff had been the only thing that had stopped her. With our dad the Angel's Halo MC president, Lexa hooking up with the law hadn't been the smartest decision she'd ever made.

But Dad eventually realized having Ben in the family was a good thing. My brother-in-law would break every law known to man if it meant protecting Lexa and making her happy. He'd covered up shit left and right since she'd told him she loved him. For her, Mom, the MC.

Me.

Killing a man and having the sheriff cover it up was one thing, especially when that man had been Carlo Santino.

Ben finding out I had an underage girl in my apartment? Probably not so much.

Fuck, who was I kidding? If Mom or Lexa found out I had an underage girl in my apartment, they would murder me.

Thankfully, I didn't have to worry about that. Delaney was eighteen. No one would come after me with a sawed-off shotgun.

I pushed my plate away and gave her my undivided attention. "You've been on the streets for ten weeks?"

She shrugged, using her fork to pick at her lasagna.

Grasping her chin, I tipped her head back so she had to look at me. "Did your aunt and uncle do anything to hurt you?" I asked between clenched teeth as I signed.

She was quick to shake her head, but there was something in her pretty eyes that told me different.

"Then why did you run?" I demanded.

Tears filled her eyes. I felt like an asshole for making her cry, but I needed answers. If someone had harmed her, they would be meeting the angel of death very, very soon. There was no fucking way I would let anyone who hurt her breathe another day.

"Marta, their housekeeper…she told me to run," she responded after a moment. "She didn't tell me why. But I knew. Uncle Tony isn't a good person. The people who came to the house…" She shuddered again. "I don't know who they were. They always kept me in my room when I wasn't at school. But I could just tell…you know?"

I tilted my head to the side as I studied her. "You were scared of your uncle, but not of me?"

She shook her head. "You won't hurt me. I can feel it. Here." She touched her hand to the center of her chest.

I wanted to laugh, but I stopped myself before the sound could leave me. She couldn't hear it if I did, but that was beside the point. She could feel me in her chest just as I could feel her in my own.

Anyone who didn't know me usually cowered when they first saw me. When they found out who I was, they damn near pissed themselves. I'd been patched into the MC the same day I turned eighteen. No need to prospect, because I'd already proven myself to my dad and his brothers. I'd already spilled blood for them and my family. Killing Carlo Santino had given me instant respect within the club.

That respect only caused others to fear me. If I'd been patched in so easily, then I must be a dangerous motherfucker.

And they were right. I would put a bullet in anyone without so much as a blink if I thought they were a danger to those I cared about.

Yet Delaney felt none of that fear when she looked at me. But she was right, too. I would gut anyone who harmed her, including myself. There was nowhere safer for this girl than with me.

3

DELANEY

Wɪᴛʜ ᴍʏ sᴛᴏᴍᴀᴄʜ ғᴜʟʟ ᴀɴᴅ ᴍʏ ʙᴏᴅʏ ʀᴇʟᴀxᴇᴅ ᴀғᴛᴇʀ ᴛʜᴇ heat of the shower, it was hard to keep my eyes open after eating the last bite of the yummy lemon cake Max said his aunt had made for him. The woman had some amazing baking skills, and I now had a new favorite dessert.

My eyes began to drift closed without my permission, and suddenly I was being lifted. Looking up at Max, I willed my heart not to jump out of my chest as I met his intense metallic gaze. "I got you, little one," I read his lips. "You're safe here. Sleep."

Closing my eyes again, I let my head rest on his chest as he carried me through the apartment. Moments later, I felt the coolness of sheets and a plush pillow under my head. My lashes flickered up to take in my surroundings. A lamp had been switched on beside the bed, casting a soft glow across the room.

The bed was a queen with a dark wooden frame. The sheets, pillowcases, and comforter were a deep crimson color. A digital clock on the nightstand beside the lamp told me it was one o'clock. Max's scent enveloped me as he tucked the comforter up around me, and I snuggled deeper into the pillow.

Before he straightened, he brushed his lips over my forehead. The sweet, innocent touch of his lips to my brow made my heart skip a beat even as tears stung my eyes. I couldn't remember the last time someone had tucked me in. By the time my parents died, I'd been putting myself to bed for a few years.

When he straightened, I was scared he was going to leave me, and I quickly caught his hand. His brows pulled together as he looked down at me. "Don't be scared," he signed.

I shook my head. "I'm not. I…" I hesitated. How did I tell him I wanted him to sleep beside me all night? I felt the safest when he was right next to me. The fear that Uncle Tony would find me had vanished, and all I felt was the kind of peace that had been missing from my life for the past eight years.

Max brushed my hair away from my face, something he'd done several times earlier. The soft sweep of his fingers across my cheek made my entire body heat as an ache throbbed between my legs. It was uncomfortable, and I pressed my legs together, trying to relieve it, only to feel a dampness on my inner thighs.

He lowered his eyes to where I was squirming, and his nostrils flared. One of his hands rubbed over his mouth as hunger filled his gaze. That only made the throb intensify, which caused me to squirm even more.

Dropping to his knees beside the bed, he cupped the side of my face, his thumb brushing over my bottom lip for several excruciating moments. "Do you ache, little one?" he signed, and I quickly nodded. "Me too, baby. But I don't think you are ready for that. I want nothing more than to crawl into this bed beside you and kiss every inch of your sweet body. I would spend the entire night easing that ache deep between your legs. And one day, I pray you'll let me. When you're ready."

"Max." My lips formed his name, but I didn't feel the vibrations in my throat that told me any sound had escaped. Still, his eyes were glued to my mouth, so I knew he understood the plea of my speaking his name.

He leaned in close, lightly touching his lips to my temple, then down to the corner of my mouth. The heat of his breath on my skin made me shiver, and I clenched my legs closed as the throb pulsed to the out-of-control beat of my heart. "Sleep," he signed. "I don't want you to have any regrets. When you're ready, I'll give you everything you want and need. I promise."

I liked that he wasn't rushing me, that he was giving me time to trust him. But for some reason, I already trusted him. More so than any other person in years. I couldn't put it into words, but there was just something in Max's eyes that told me every part of myself was safe with this guy.

Including my heart.

But even though my entire body was one achy throb, I wasn't sure if I was ready for that kind of intimacy. I was a virgin. Did guys even want a virgin these days? One of the girls at school had been telling her friends that she'd had sex with her boyfriend. He'd gotten so pissed because it was her first time and he'd thought she was more experienced, that he'd actually broken up with her over it.

I'd thought the guy was a douchebag, that he'd only been after sex and once he'd gotten it, he'd come up with whatever dumb reason to break up with her. But now, I wondered if Max would get upset that I had no experience. Would he still want me if he knew? Would it turn him off?

He tapped me on the nose, pulling me out of my thoughts. "Sleep," he encouraged. "I'll be on the couch."

Quickly, I sat up, shaking my head. If anyone should be on the couch, it was me. He'd already given me so much. A delicious meal. A hot shower. Fresh clothes. A roof over my head. And now I was taking up his bed? It wasn't right to steal his big comfy bed as well.

He gently pushed me back down until my head was resting on the pillows. "You are going to sleep in here," he signed while glaring down at me. "I need you to sleep in my bed, little one."

"But—"

He captured my hands before I could sign more and kissed each palm before tucking them under the blanket. "Don't argue. I won't sleep if you don't take the bed, and I have to work in the morning."

"Where do you work?" I asked curiously.

"Downstairs," he informed me with a shrug. "My dad owns half of the garage. I'll inherit it one day, which was why he didn't argue when I told him I was moving out and into this place." He tucked the covers around me again, then leaned forward and rubbed my nose with his. "Sweet dreams, little treasure."

Despite the lingering ache between my legs, I was almost asleep before he even closed the bedroom door on his way out. The bed was just too comfy and warm. With his scent surrounding me, and knowing he was just a room away, my brain shut down and sleep pulled me under.

The next time I opened my eyes, the sun was shining through the window. A glance at the clock told me it was 11:32. Gasping, I sat upright in bed. I hadn't slept so late since leaving Uncle Tony's house, and even then, it was a rare occurrence. Marta usually woke me up with breakfast, no matter what day of the week it was.

As I leaned back against the headboard, my fingers brushed over a sheet of paper. Picking it up, I saw it was a note from Max. Seeing his somewhat messy, masculine handwriting made me smile.

Delaney,

I didn't want to leave for work without letting you know, but you were sleeping so peacefully I didn't have the heart to wake you. I'll come up for lunch, and we can eat together. Make yourself at home, because that is exactly what it is for you now.

There is cereal and other breakfast food in the pantry. The coffeepot is ready to go. Just turn it on when you get up.

See you soon, little one.

Max

I traced a fingertip over his name, a smile teasing at the corners of my mouth. Could he be any sweeter?

I tucked the note against my chest for a moment, my heart melting for him. Was it insane that I was falling for a guy I'd only met the night before? Maybe, but I realized I didn't care if I was crazy or not. I liked Max, and with the way he made my heart so dang happy, I knew I could fall in love with him all too easily.

That should scare me, but fear was the last thing he made me feel.

Folding the piece of paper, I tucked it under my pillow and then got out of bed. I used the bathroom and saw that Max had left an extra toothbrush on the sink for me. I unwrapped it and placed it beside his in the holder. The sight made my heart constrict with a shot of pure happiness, and I practically skipped into the kitchen.

I made coffee and then a slice of toast. If Max was coming back for lunch, I wanted to eat with him, but my stomach was already vibrating with grumbles, demanding some kind of peace offering to hold it over until he returned.

After eating and savoring a cup of coffee, I cleaned up the kitchen and then went to take another shower. I'd had to wash my hair three times the night before just to feel clean, but I still washed it again. I needed to shave, but I didn't want to ruin Max's razor. Maybe I could find a job so I could buy a few personal items.

My period was due, and I'd run out of the hygiene products Marta had given me. I'd stocked up some at the shelters I'd stayed in back in Oakland, but those hadn't lasted long either. Deciding I'd worry about that when the time came, I finished washing my body and then stepped out of the stall.

As I was wrapping the towel around myself, the bathroom door opened. My gaze locked with Max's, and his nostrils flared. Hungrily, his metallic eyes caressed my body, his eyes tracing droplets of water as they dripped down my neck and were absorbed by the thick towel.

He tipped his head back for a moment, and I quickly made sure the towel was in place before he lowered his gaze back to mine. "Hi," he greeted with a smile. "Did you miss me?"

I nodded, my own eyes eating up the sight of him. He was wearing dark-wash jeans again, but instead of the leather vest —or cut as he'd explained to me the night before—and white T-shirt, he was wearing a black industrial-style button-up. The sleeves were tight over his upper arms and molded to his thick chest. I was so entranced by the sight of him, I didn't have time to feel embarrassed that I stood there with hairy legs.

"Good," he signed. "You finish up in here, and I'll make us some sandwiches."

I nodded again, but I couldn't take my eyes off him. He seemed to have the same problem, because he stood there for another minute before cupping the side of my face. I leaned into his touch, savoring the feel of his rough palm against my softer flesh.

"I need to feed you," I read his lips. "But first, I need to taste you."

I tilted my head back, silently giving him permission to kiss me all he wanted. He grabbed hold of my waist with his other hand, jerking me against him before cupping one of my hips. His thick fingers squeezed my bottom, and I felt my moan of pleasure vibrate in my chest. Slowly, I watched as his head lowered.

The kiss started off gentle, as if he were afraid of scaring me. But when my lips slightly parted, shyly offering him access, it changed. His fingers squeezed my hip, massaging it as his tongue stabbed in and out of my mouth, playing with my own.

When he finally lifted his head, we were both breathing hard and my mouth tingled. Touching my finger to it, I tried to press the feeling deeper, wanting it to linger, but he caught my hand and pulled it away. Dropping a softer yet quick kiss on my lips, he stepped back. "I need you to hurry and get dressed, little treasure," he signed, his movements urgent. "Before I do something that might mess this up."

Before I could assure him he wouldn't mess anything up, he turned and closed the door as he left.

4

———

MAX

As soon as she walked into the kitchen, I wanted to grab her and spread her across the island. Maybe eating Delaney for lunch would help me focus on work instead of just lying beneath the car I was supposed to be fixing, thinking about how much I missed her.

It seemed ridiculous to miss her when she was so close, but I fucking did. Badly. That pressure in my chest had only gotten worse and worse as the morning had gone on and I couldn't see or touch her. As soon as it was noon, I'd called to my dad that I was going to grab something to eat, and I'd hauled ass up the side steps to my apartment. Luckily, he'd been on his way home himself to eat with Mom, or he probably would have stopped me.

And I honestly didn't know what I would have done if he or anyone else had delayed me from seeing my little treasure.

She was wearing another one of my T-shirts and a pair of my old sweats. They swallowed her whole, making her look even smaller than she was, and I fucking loved it. Her hands landed on the island where I was finishing up with our sandwiches, and I glanced down, spotting her injured finger.

Dropping the butter knife into the mayo jar, I turned and washed my hands before grabbing the first aid box off the top of the fridge. I'd forgotten about the wound on her finger, and it pissed me off. I should have taken care of it the night before. The first time I'd noticed it, I could tell it was infected and painful for her.

She frowned until I took her hand in mine and carefully cleaned the nailless finger. She flinched when the alcohol swab brushed over the reddened flesh, but she clenched her jaw and didn't pull away. Meanwhile, I began to sweat because I knew my doctoring was causing her discomfort. The thought of her in pain drove me crazy. Knowing I was the cause of that pain pushed me to the brink.

As if she knew my inner struggle, she touched my back with her other hand and leaned her head against my arm. I brushed a kiss over her brow before finally tossing the little gauze in the trash and then slathering a little antibiotic ointment over the area before bandaging it.

Once it was covered, I lifted her hand and kissed her fingertip, earning me a sweet smile from her sexy lips. She wrapped her arms around my middle and tilted her head back. Unable to stop myself, I bent and brushed my lips over hers. It was a soft kiss, barely a flutter of our mouths touching, but it got me harder than I'd ever been in my life.

Her sigh did nothing to calm the inferno she was causing within me. Lifting her, I placed her on the island and then finished making our lunch. Picking up half of the ham and turkey sandwich, I touched it to her lips, and she took a small bite.

"What's your favorite sandwich?" I asked once my hands were free.

Her brow scrunched up as she considered her answer.

"Grilled cheese," she signed, then added. "But peanut butter and jelly is a close second."

I grimaced. "Sorry, baby. You won't find anything peanut butter in this place. My sister is allergic."

"That's okay. I like BLTs just as much." She took a hungry bite of her sandwich.

"I'll make sure I get bacon at the grocery store," I promised, then wiped my mouth on a paper towel. "I'm going to grab you a few things after I pick up Nova later. Can you tell me what sizes you wear?"

She seemed to deflate right in front of my eyes, and I replayed what I'd just said that could have caused that kind of reaction. When it hit me, I stepped between her legs. "Nova is my cousin," I told her with a grin. "She's thirteen and like another sister to me. I'll bring her back with me so you can meet her."

Her brown eyes brightened, and for the first time, I noticed there were flecks of green scattered within them. I became hypnotized by the discovery and realized there was more green in her left eye than her right.

Delaney stroked her fingertips down my jaw, a smile teasing at her lips as they brushed through the two-day-old scruff. "You don't have to buy me things. I was going to ask if you knew anywhere I could get a job." She sucked her bottom lip into her mouth before continuing. "Maybe somewhere that will pay in cash? I don't want my uncle to find me by creating a paper trail."

"We can talk about that later," I deflected. "And I want to buy you a few things. As much as I love seeing you in my clothes, eventually my family will want to meet you. I don't want to have to rip Reid's eyeballs out of his head if he sees you without a bra on."

Her skin glowed a pretty pink. "I will pay you back."

"No," I growled, even though I knew she couldn't hear it. "You will not."

"But, Max—"

I caught hold of her hands and wrapped them around my waist, putting an end to the argument before it even got started. "I want to know your sizes and what your favorite colors are. Write them down for me before I go back to work. I have watch duty at the middle school today, and I usually pick up Nova when it's my turn."

She only glared up at me, but I gave her a quick kiss. "Please, little treasure," I signed with a pout. "Let me take care of you."

"You have already given me so much," she said after pulling her hands free. "I don't want to take advantage of your kindness."

I threw back my head and laughed, which earned me a light slap to the chest. Grinning, I shook my head at how adorable she was. "No one has ever called me kind before, treasure. Not even my own mother. But I really like that you think I am."

She rolled her eyes at me. Laughing, I tickled her until she was squealing and giggling, begging me to stop. Her giggles and her voice as she cried "stop" were the sweetest, most precious sounds I'd ever heard. I hated that she couldn't hear it or my own voice, but I was just thankful the accident that had taken her ability to hear hadn't robbed me of her as well.

After lunch—and I'd gotten her to write down her sizes and favorite colors—I left her with a kiss to her soft lips and a promise to bring home dinner. The kiss would have to hold me over until I got back, but I wasn't confident it would help any.

Somehow, I was able to finish up the repairs to the car I

was working on before I had to ride over to the middle school. Ever since two of Ramirez's men had attacked Nova to send a message to the Vitucci family, the MC had been taking shifts each morning and afternoon at all three of the schools in town to make sure that she and the other students stayed safe.

I watched over the middle school three days a week in the afternoon with my cousin Reid. For me, it had been a toss-up between wanting to watch over the high school because of my cousin River or the middle school for Nova. But since River's boyfriend took both the morning and afternoon shifts for the high school, I decided Nova needed me more.

Pulling up in front of the school, I gave a chin lift to some of the parents I knew who were already in the parent pickup line. Reid arrived a few minutes later. Turning off his motor-cycle, he took off his helmet and shook his head as his gaze drifted over the scratches on the side of my bike.

"What the fuck happened?"

I shrugged and told him the same story I'd given my dad when he'd asked that exact question earlier. "There was this huge-ass elk in the road last night. Didn't see it until I was right up on it because of the fog. Figured if I hit it, one of us wouldn't walk away from the collision, and I wasn't too confident it would be me. Ended up swerving and wiped out."

"Fuck, man," Reid muttered. "You okay?"

"Just a little road rash and a few sore muscles. I'll live. Don't tell my mom, though. I don't want to worry her."

My cousin nodded, his blue eyes, a Reid family trade-mark, glowing with understanding. Reid's last name should have been Reid, but his mom had kept his birth a secret from his dad for the first two years of his life. When they got married, his dad hadn't wanted to saddle him with the name Reid Reid, so they hadn't changed it from Reid Barker. And since their construction company was Barker & Reid Construction and he was going to inherit part of it regardless, there was no reason to worry about it.

"Don't worry, cuz. I got your back."

The bell rang, announcing the end of the school day. Slowly, kids started trickling out of the school and got into their parents' vehicles. When Nova walked out, her backpack tossed over one shoulder, she gave me a tight smile and climbed on my bike behind me.

Reid and I shared a look before turning our attention to my little cousin. I shifted so I could look at her. Every time I set eyes on Nova, my heart gave a little squeeze. She was a tiny little replica of my mom. Even her attitude was just like Raven Hannigan Reid's at times.

"What's wrong?" I demanded. "Someone being mean to you? Do I need to kick some little asses?"

She rolled her green eyes. "No, dummy."

"Then what's wrong?" Reid asked, his tone less aggressive than my own—slightly. "You're obviously upset about something."

Her shoulders slumped. "Ryan's going to kill Garret."

I glanced at Reid, and then we both burst out laughing. "Let him," I told her. "That fucking asshole needs a good ass-beating."

"Just out of curiosity, what did your idiot brother do this time?" Reid inquired, his brows lifted. "Uncle Jet mentioned Ryan practically choking Garret out when he got here last week. All I'm saying about that is, I wouldn't have had as much restraint. I wanted to put my boot up that little fucker's ass too. He should have been there to protect you."

She mumbled something I didn't catch, and I reached out, tugging on her blond ponytail. "Speak up."

She slapped my hand away. "He's been baiting Ramirez,"

she repeated. "On social media. Ramirez's stepdaughter, or whatever the hell she is, has a huge following on her Instagram, and Garret has been taunting him on her page."

"Does he want to get you killed?" I growled. Turning, I started my bike. There were no parents in line any longer, so I knew Reid could handle the rest of our shift on his own. "You don't have to worry about Ryan killing the little fucker, Nova. Because I'm going to put a bullet in him."

"No!" she cried, grabbing hold of my arm and tugging on it until I turned my head to look at her over my shoulder. "Please, Max. He doesn't even understand the kind of trouble he's stirring up. Let me—"

"What?" I snapped. "Let you coddle him? One day, you're going to realize that you can't protect your brother forever, sweetheart. He has to take responsibility for his own actions eventually. And I'd rather he not learn that lesson because he got you killed."

Nova exhaled heavily and glanced off into the distance for a moment before turning her gaze back to mine. "I know. But I can't help wanting to protect him."

"Ah, Nova. It should be the other way around. He should be the one protecting you, honey. You're the precious one. But all he cares about is himself."

Tears filled her eyes, but she blinked them back, refusing to allow a single one to spill over her lashes. "I know, but I keep hoping he will change." Swallowing hard, she put her hands at my waist. "Can we please just go?" She glanced at Reid then back to me. I'd texted her earlier to ask if she would help me shop for Delaney. She knew she was the only person I'd told about my little treasure. I could trust Nova to keep any secret I asked her to. Like my mom, she was loyal to a fault. "I need to pick up a few things at the store. Do you mind taking me shopping?"

"You two go on," Reid urged. "I got this covered. It's only going to be a few more minutes before the teachers leave anyway."

I gave him a nod in thanks, and Nova tightened her hold. With her backpack slung over both shoulders now and my extra helmet on her head, she was as secure as she could get. Her dad had been letting her ride on the back of his own bike since she was three, so it was as normal to her as breathing.

There weren't many places to shop for nice clothes in Creswell Springs. River and Mila were opening their own store to cater to a woman's every need, Womanland, but it wouldn't be open for a few more weeks. I didn't want to waste time driving the hour to the nearest mall, even though I knew I could get Delaney better clothes there.

Promising myself I would take her on a shopping spree soon, I let Nova loose in the one little boutique. She knew women's clothes better than I did, so I was going to trust her judgment on anything she chose for my little treasure.

Two hours later, with several bags of clothes, shoes, and other essentials, we picked up dinner at Aggie's and then went back to my place.

As soon as I opened the door to my apartment, I felt Delaney's presence, and the pressure in my chest eased some-what. When I spotted her curled up on the couch with a blanket tucked around her as she read one of the books Nova had left the last time she'd visited me, the pressure all but disappeared.

Dropping the bags of clothes on the floor, I scooped Delaney up and pressed my forehead to hers. She practically purred as she cuddled against me. We stayed just like that for several long moments before Nova cleared her throat, reminding me she was there.

I lifted my head, noting that she was holding the two

takeout bags while she skimmed her eyes over the girl in my arms. Her lips tilted up in a smile as she used her foot to close the front door and walked over to us. Delaney's head snapped around, her eyes taking in my little cousin curiously as her cheeks glowed a soft pink with shyness.

Setting the bags on the coffee table, Nova introduced herself. "Hi, Delaney," she signed. Nova was a genius when it came to learning new languages. She was fluent in Italian, Russian, and Spanish. American Sign Language, Mom had been teaching her from birth, just as she had Lexa and me. "I'm Nova."

My girl squirmed until I set her on her feet, and she held out her hand. Nova smiled as she shook it.

"You're as beautiful as Max said you would be." Delaney blushed and melted against me once more. "Honestly, I thought he was exaggerating, but for once, he spoke the complete truth."

I glared at Nova. "Shut up, kid. Before she thinks I'm a liar."

Nova giggled, her eyes sparkling with amusement. I was just glad to see that she wasn't upset over the whole Garret thing for the moment. "I'm kidding. There's no one I trust more than Max to tell it to me straight."

Delaney glanced up at me, and the look in her pretty brown eyes had me catching my breath. "I already knew that," she told Nova.

I dropped a kiss on the tip of her nose, then nudged her toward the kitchen. "Let's eat before the food gets cold."

Nova scooped up the bags again and followed us into the next room. While I got drinks, she pulled out the containers of food. I hadn't known what Delaney would like, so I'd gone simple with cheeseburgers and fries for all three of us. When she opened her box, her eyes got huge and she did a little happy dance, and I was glad I'd picked correctly.

Her moan at the first big bite she took went straight to my dick, and I was glad the island was between my cousin and me because I didn't want her to see the bulge that was now straining the confines of my jeans. Between bites, Delaney and Nova got to know each other, and I just stood back and watched the two of them.

My cousin seemed to adore Delaney, and I was hoping Lexa and Mom felt the same instant connection. Not that it would stop what was going to happen between this little treasure and me if they didn't, but it would make things easier on my girl. Around eight, Aunt Flick honked the horn of her SUV from the garage's parking lot.

Nova gave Delaney a hug then motioned for me to follow her out as she gathered her stuff.

I walked out the door with her, and she turned to face me with a frown. "You know she's the girl Maverick has been looking for, right?"

I clenched my jaw and nodded. I'd known that from the moment I'd brought her home, and that was why I hadn't wanted to take Delaney shopping yet. Ben had gotten calls about someone breaking in to local businesses, and then Maverick had told us that River suspected it was a girl who had also gotten into the Ink Shoppe a few times. But nothing had been stolen—not even food, from what my brother-in-law had said—so Delaney hadn't really broken any laws. And even if she had, I wasn't about to let her be arrested. Ben and Maverick didn't need to know the girl had been found.

Nova's face softened. "Don't worry. I won't tell anyone. She's so sweet, Max. I love her already." She punched me in the arm before pointing her finger up at me. "You better take good care of her, or I swear I'll kick your ass."

I laughed and bent to kiss the top of her head. "Easy, little lioness. No need to get violent. I promise I'll take care of my treasure."

"That is so adorable," she gushed. Throwing her arms around my middle, she gave me a quick squeeze before turning to descend the stairs. "Text me if you need anything. Love you."

"Love you too, Nova," I called after her, then waited until she texted me she was in the SUV before going back inside.

Delaney was right where I left her, cuddled up on the couch once again, with a blanket tucked around her legs. I hadn't shown her what was in the shopping bags yet, mostly because I wanted her to try everything on for me, and I didn't want Nova to witness how my body was going to respond to the show.

Once the door was securely locked behind me, I grabbed the bags and carried them into the bedroom before coming back and scooping her into my arms. She giggled and clung to me as I carried her into our bedroom and placed her in the center of the bed.

"It's not much," I told her. "This town doesn't really have a lot to offer for fashion yet. But once you're settled in, we can go to the mall and get you whatever you want."

"You didn't have to do this," she argued. "I'm fine with your clothes."

"But I want you to have pretty things," I signed before pouring out the contents of the first bag onto the bed in front of her. There were a few pairs of jeans that she said were her size, several tops in different styles, panties, and bras. All of which Nova had picked out.

While she shifted through the clothes, I grabbed the other bags, the ones from the grocery store. They held shampoo, conditioner, body wash, and deodorant that Nova had also picked out, along with a few other items I'd trusted my cousin about when she'd said Delaney would need them. I grabbed the box of tampons and the package of other feminine hygiene products, intending to put them in the bathroom, but my girl's eyes widened and then filled with tears.

I dropped them on the floor and reached for her. "What's wrong?" I demanded, the pressure returning to my chest.

"You." She signed as her tears fell faster. "You're too much."

My heart stopped. "I'm sorry. I'll fix it. Just tell me what I did wrong."

Delaney shook her head. "No. You did nothing wrong. You are…perfect."

Her answer only confused me. "Then why are you crying, treasure?"

A sob escaped her, and she burrowed her face into my chest for a moment. But I couldn't fucking breathe. Cupping the side of her face, I tipped her head back and repeated the question slowly so she could read my lips. "Why are you crying, baby?"

"Because I'm happy, and that scares me. The last time I was happy, I lost my parents." She began to tremble as she fought to contain her sobs while still signing the next words. "And I don't want to lose you, Max."

5

———

DELANEY

How could one person change my entire world in less than twenty-four hours?

I'd gone from having nothing and no one, to Max giving me everything. It felt like a dream. Someone cared about me, and that meant more to me than anything in the world.

The last time someone had cared, I'd lost them both in the blink of an eye. Max was quickly becoming so much more than just the hero who rescued me the night before. I was feeling things I'd never felt before for anyone. It was exhilarating—but yeah, totally terrifying.

If I allowed myself to get too close and then I lost Max, it would destroy me completely.

Yet, I wasn't sure I even cared.

All I wanted was to savor whatever this was with him.

He stroked my hair back from my tear-soaked face and placed a tender kiss on my forehead. That simple, innocent touch of his lips on my skin was enough to calm the sobs trying to tear me apart, and I blinked up at him in an attempt to stop the flood of tears from my eyes.

"You will never lose me," he signed with a look on his

face that told me he meant every word. "Because I am never, ever, letting you go, little treasure."

My heart melted as he called me that sweet endearment yet again. The first time, I'd tried to ignore the puddle of goo it turned me into, thinking maybe he was just being kind. But I was starting to think he really did consider me his treasure. I didn't understand how this hot, amazing guy would want me, but I didn't want to open his eyes to the reality of how messed up I was either.

Picking me up, he sat on the edge of the bed and cradled me in his arms. I rested my head on his chest and inhaled deeply, taking in the scent of cedar and citrus along with the hint of what must have been oil from the car he'd worked on earlier. The scent soothed something deep in my soul, and I closed my eyes, just letting myself enjoy being in his arms for the moment.

I couldn't hear the beating of his heart, but I could feel it through his shirt, telling me it was pounding erratically. Concerned, I lifted my head to ask if he was okay.

As soon as our gazes locked, he was devouring me in a kiss that left me breathless and achy. He'd given me my first kiss, but I was a quick learner and I kissed him back, wanting to taste and please him just as he did me with the simple brush of his tongue over mine.

His hands dropped to my behind and lifted my legs until I was straddling his hips on the bed. I felt the vibrations from his deep groan as he kissed his way from my lips to my jaw and then down my neck. I arched, willingly giving him better access as his teeth scraped over my flesh, causing goose bumps to pop up everywhere he touched.

I felt something hard and hot pulse against my inner thigh, and I shifted until that hardness was pressed right where I ached the most. Sounds I couldn't name left my throat. I couldn't hear them, but the way Max's eyes glittered told me he liked the sounds I was making.

My hands went to his throat, wanting to feel the vibrations when he made noises as well. I shifted my hips, rubbing my pulsing center over his thick hardness through our layers of clothes. The vibrations from his throat were long and made my fingertips tingle. My nipples pebbled even harder than they already were, and I pressed my chest to his as I rubbed myself against him like a cat wanting to be petted.

But then he was grasping my hands and pulling them behind my back as his lips slowly formed words so I could read what he was saying. "Hold that thought, little treasure," he said with a wink.

Shifting, he pulled his phone from his front jeans pocket. Glancing down at the screen, he grimaced, and I caught sight of the name "Prez" before he lifted it to his ear. As he answered, he turned his head away, and my heart sank. Obviously, he didn't want me to know what he was talking about, and that…hurt.

It shouldn't. He had every right to his privacy. I was an interloper after all. But Max had been so kind and included me in so much already that it was wrenching to realize he didn't trust me as much as I already trusted him.

When I got off his lap, his hand caught my hip and squeezed for a second before releasing me, continuing to keep his head turned away. I watched him for a few moments, noticing how tense his shoulders got the longer he stayed on the phone. Not wanting to add more stress to him, I started folding the clothes he'd so kindly bought for me and placed them in the corner of the room so they weren't in the way.

Keeping busy left him out of my line of sight, so I was startled when his arms wrapped around me from behind, and I felt his lips touch my shoulder. I felt him inhale deeply before turning me to face him.

"I have to go take care of something for my dad," he signed, his face tight, almost angry. "I don't know how late I'll be out." Taking my hand, he pulled me over to the bed and pushed me down. Then he just turned and walked away.

I sat there, unsure of what to do. He hadn't even said goodbye…

Just as my heart was squeezing painfully, Max reappeared with a smaller bag in his hand. Crouching down in front of me, he pulled out a rectangular box, and my mouth fell open. Opening the box, he lifted out a phone that looked just like his own, but instead of black, this one was a pretty baby blue.

"All that has been set up is my contact information. I'll text you Nova's number later." He placed the phone in my hand, his eyes having lost some of the anger I'd seen right after he'd gotten off the phone.

"This…is…mine?" I signed, so shocked, all I could do was gaze from him to the phone and back again.

I'd never had a phone before. My parents had decided I was old enough on our trip to Belize, and they had said they would get me one as soon as we got home. But then the explosion happened. When I moved in with Aunt June and Uncle Tony, they hadn't offered, and I wasn't allowed out of my room except to go to school, so it wasn't like I could ask.

Not that I would have. I hadn't wanted to draw any kind of attention to myself from either of them. Even back then, I'd sensed something off with those two.

"Yes, treasure," Max told me, his jaw clenching. "And don't argue with me about it. I need to be able to contact you when I'm not with you. Not being able to check in on you this evening was pure hell. I've set the ring to the highest vibration, so you should be able to feel it when you get an alert. I'm not much of a texter, but if it means I have a way of communicating with you when we're apart, then I'll be the king of texting."

The seriousness on his face made me smile. "You shouldn't have done this," I told him. He started to tell me not to argue again, but I quickly went on. "I love it. Thank you. I don't know how to use it, but I will learn. For you."

"You don't know how…?" He spoke the words with a dark frown on his beautiful face before signing, "You've never had a phone before?"

Feeling my cheeks turning pink with embarrassment, I shook my head.

"Let me give you a quick lesson." He showed me how to turn it off and on. Then how to send a text. He brought up his contact information and sent himself a message so that I could see how it worked.

Once I assured him I could do it myself now, he stood and brushed his lips over my brow. "I don't know what time I will be back. If you need anything, text me." I nodded and gave him a small smile as he grabbed his leather MC vest. His metallic-blue gaze lingered on me, before he clenched his jaw. "I will try to make this as quick as possible."

"Go," I urged. "I will be fine."

Another gentle kiss to my forehead and he was gone. I sat there for a long time, just watching the door, wondering what he was going to do. He hadn't been happy about leaving, and even though I had no idea what the phone call had been about, I'd noticed how tense he'd been during it. It was obvious he didn't want to do whatever it was he needed to.

I wasn't sure how long I just sat there, holding my phone and watching the doorway to the bedroom, hoping he would come back. The little device vibrated in my hand, hard, and I looked down to see a text from him.

MyMax was what he'd programmed his contact name as, and seeing it on the screen lifted my heart.

MyMax: *This is going to take a few hours to clean up. Get comfortable, treasure. Sorry I won't get to tuck you in tonight.*

Clean up? I felt something ease deep inside me. When he'd turned away during his conversation, maybe it had been because he was frustrated he had to clean up some kind of huge mess. I could understand that. He'd worked all day and then gone shopping for me. He was probably exhausted.

Heart feeling lighter suddenly, I texted him back.

Me: *I'll wait up for you.*

MyMax: *No, baby. I want you to sleep. Play with your phone for a while. There is an Apple Books app that Nova said has tons of free books. I'll set you up an account tomorrow so you can buy whatever you want. And there are games in the app store you might like. Have fun, but don't stay up too late.*

I started to type out an argument, telling him I would wait up for him again, when another text came in from him.

MyMax: *I miss you already. Knowing you're at home safe in our bed is all that is keeping me from saying to hell with this shit. Get some sleep. For me, treasure.*

Well, dang, I mused as I gazed down at the phone in my hand. How could I possibly argue with that?

Me: *I miss you too. Don't work too hard. Xo*

That got me a red heart emoji in response, which put a goofy smile on my face. Dropping back onto the bed, I held the phone to my chest. Max Reid was turning out to be the hero prince in all of those fairy tales I used to love to read when I was a kid. I didn't think guys like that really existed, yet I'd found one and he was treating me like I truly was his treasure.

Happily, I rolled onto my side and came face-to-face with all kinds of girlie bathroom items.

Gasping, I sat up and inspected everything. Realizing I now had the tools to groom everything that needed attention, I gathered them and my phone and rushed into the bathroom.

Maybe it was a good thing Max had been called out. Now, I had time to take care of my legs and other areas so that the next time we kissed I wouldn't be embarrassed to take things further.

And I ached to take them so much further.

6

MAX

MY FIST CONNECTED WITH THE BASTARD'S GUT SO HARD, THE contents of his stomach spewed from his mouth. If I'd been standing in front of him and not to the side, I would have been covered in his puke. Which would have had me ending this sooner than I knew my dad wanted—without getting the information he was interested in—because I would have put a bullet in the motherfucker's head.

I couldn't go home with puke all over me. Blood might be something I could come up with a cover story to tell Delaney that wouldn't make her scared of me. Hell, it might even get me sympathy from her since this was taking so much longer than I had first anticipated.

When Dad called and said he needed me to help Uncle Spider deal with someone, I'd been pissed. Delaney had been in my lap, her wet little pussy soaking through the sweats she was wearing. The feel and scent had been enough to make me come a little in my jeans, and I'd been seconds away from rolling her onto her back and burying my face between her thighs.

But I couldn't tell him that. For one, I didn't want him or

anyone else to know about my little treasure until she trusted me completely. So far, it had been easier than I'd thought, which was a good thing. I didn't want to mess up the progress I'd already made with her. I just wanted her in love with me before I introduced her to my parents so that she wouldn't want to leave me once she realized Mom could be a little… intense at times.

Especially when she was trying to protect those she loved.

I knew she would love Delaney, but would it freak my girl out at how Mom tended to show her love?

Delaney was on the run from her family, who she said were bad people. And my fear was that maybe she would get the wrong impression of Mom once she realized that Raven Hannigan Reid's go-to way of showing affection was putting a gun to the head of anyone she deemed a threat to her babies.

Uncle Spider motioned for me to back away as the guy who'd just blown chunks groaned and coughed. He was a mess, with blood and sweat dripping from his brow. His eyes were bloodshot from pain, but I wouldn't have been surprised if this idiot was high on something hard. It would explain why he hadn't broken yet. The drugs were dulling the pain I was dishing out.

And I'd already dished out a hell of a lot.

His left eye was swelling shut, and his nose was broken, the blood steadily streaming out. I'd taken off my cut and shirt before I'd started beating him, but my jeans still had droplets on them. My fists were cracked in a few places, but I'd put on gloves so his blood didn't mix with mine. No fucking way was I chancing this guy was carrying something I couldn't get rid of.

The puke had a few pieces of broken teeth in it, which didn't surprise me. I had a powerful uppercut. I was honestly surprised I hadn't knocked him out from all the punches to the head he'd already sustained.

"I'm going to ask you again," Uncle Spider said in his deceptively soft voice. That tone made me have to fight a shiver. The enforcer used that voice to fuck with his prey, get them to think they could trust him, before he struck. The last time I'd heard him use it, he'd gotten some poor bastard to spill every secret he'd ever kept all the way back to childhood. Then Uncle Spider had slit the sobbing fool's throat without flinching. The shock and betrayal on the guy's face when the room filled with gurgling sounds as he fought for breath that wouldn't come while he choked on his own blood was something I wouldn't forget. "Why were you creeping around town?"

"Just enjoying the scenery, man," his newest victim said with a laugh. "Ain't no crime in that, is there?"

Maybe not in other towns, it wasn't, but in Creswell Springs, when a stranger caught the eye of the Angel's Halo MC prez, and he didn't like what he saw—or he felt like the stranger was a threat—it was grounds to haul the motherfucker into this old shack and question him. So far, this one hadn't been very forthcoming. Hence, the beating he was getting.

It turned to an agonized groan when I picked up a blade and stabbed it into his right thigh. With his hands tied over his head, they took most of his weight when his knees buckled on him for a minute from the pain.

"Fuck!" he roared, his breathing coming in heavy pants now. He turned his bloodshot eyes on me and spat at my feet, earning him another punch to the face.

"Untie my hands, cocksucker," he growled. "Let's me and you do this right."

I smirked and pulled the blade from his thigh, keeping

quiet. I wasn't there to talk to him. Getting answers was Uncle Spider's job. He was the "good cop" in this little game. And when I didn't answer their taunts, that only pissed them off more. I fucking loved it.

"Who do you work for?" the enforcer asked when the guy stopped cursing so savagely at me.

"Fuck you," he seethed.

Uncle Spider sighed in disappointment. Turning, he walked over to the chair several feet away and sat. Stretching his long legs out in front of him, he crossed his arms over his chest and gave me a nod.

My smirk turned into something feral as I strolled to my long table of tools and took a moment to choose my next toy. This fucker's legs seemed to be his weakness, so I grabbed the ball bat and walked back over to him. The first strike to his left knee had him screaming even louder than when I'd stabbed him.

Without giving him time to recover, I took out his other knee. Two more slams to each leg and he was sobbing as his entire weight shifted to his arms because he could no longer stand on his own.

"Tony Garcia!" he yelled, snot mixing with the blood still coming from his nose and dripping into his puddle of puke. "He's looking for his niece. She ran away months ago, and he sent me to find her. Followed her trail close to here, then it went cold. Figured she was still in the area. That's all. I fucking swear."

I froze.

Delaney had said her uncle's name was Tony, and I didn't think it was a coincidence that there were two girls on the run from their uncle in the same town. Which meant this mother-fucker had come to take my treasure away from me.

I didn't even wait for my uncle to give me the signal. I

wasn't even thinking past the need to protect my girl as I pulled my gun and popped two in the bastard's forehead.

"The fuck, Max?" Uncle Spider grumbled.

"I believed him," I said with a shrug as I tucked the gun back into the waistband of my jeans. "Maverick and River are looking for a homeless girl. I figure that's who he's looking for."

He grunted but nodded. "Yeah. I have a feeling that's who he meant too." Standing, he frowned at the mess on the floor then at the guy hanging lifelessly in front of me. "It's Chance's and Elias's turn to clean up. I'll make sure they do it right. You head on home."

I flexed my shoulders, trying to relieve some of the tension that was starting to tighten them. "You sure? I can take care of this."

"Nah, you did plenty tonight. Good work." He picked up my shirt and tossed it to me. "Be careful. Don't want you playing chicken with another elk."

I grinned. "Ah, come on. I need a little more excitement in my life."

He shoved my arm. "Get home, boy."

I laughed and grabbed my cut on the way out the door. As soon as I pulled into the parking lot at the garage and turned off my bike, I grabbed my phone, doing a search on Tony Garcia.

The number of Tony Garcias in the state of California alone was astronomical, but I knew I'd found him as soon as I started reading his list of crimes.

"Sonofabitch," I muttered when I saw the top article about the man. He was into drugs and prostitution of underage girls. As I skimmed through other articles, I knew Delaney had every reason to fear him.

If she hadn't run, it was only a matter of time before she became one of his working girls.

I had to sit there and get control of myself before I went up to the apartment, not wanting to scare my girl with how I was shaking with rage.

In my gut, I knew I was going to have to put an end to Uncle Tony. If he had men out looking for her, then he must want to use her for something. And I would die before I let him get his filthy hands on my little treasure.

Tony Garcia's days were numbered.

7

———

DELANEY

THE FEEL OF STRONG ARMS WRAPPED AROUND ME AND WARM breath on my neck had my eyes blinking. It took a minute for my mind to clear of sleep before I could recognize my surroundings, but once I did, a smile lifted my lips and I cuddled back against Max's hard body.

I felt the vibrations of his groan through my back, and the breath on my skin became…heavier. His hold tightened, tucking me closer, and I lowered my lashes as I enjoyed just being in his arms.

So, this was what peace felt like. Wrapped in the warmth and safety of a man I knew all the way down to my soul wouldn't hurt me. With my heart light as a feather, yet a messy puddle of goo in the center of my chest. I wanted to bottle up this feeling so that I could carry it around with me everywhere I went.

My shirt had been lifted a few inches, exposing a patch of skin on my stomach. Max's fingers found it and started tracing shapes across it. A diamond. A circle. A star.

When he started tracing a heart, he kept it up until I squirmed against him. He caught my hip in his other hand

55

and held me still as he circled his groin against my backside, grinding his hardness into my hip. My breath caught at how sensual and naughty the action was.

All I was wearing was one of his T-shirts and a pair of the new panties he'd bought me. From the feel of it, all he had on was a pair of boxers or shorts. The thin material wasn't much protection for either of us, and I wanted them gone.

Suddenly, I found myself on my back with Max leaning over me. His lips slowly formed words, and with the sun shining through the window, I could easily read what he was saying. "Need to taste you, treasure. Give me permission."

Almost frantically, I started nodding. I didn't know what he meant by tasting me, but I wanted it. Ached for it.

His nostrils flared, and he pulled my borrowed shirt up over my head, leaving me lying there in only a pair of cotton bikini briefs. Those beautiful metallic-blue eyes skimmed over me, and goose bumps popped up as if he had physically caressed me. When his gaze reached my breasts, my nipples hardened painfully.

"So beautiful." Lowering his head, he captured one nipple with his mouth and sucked hard.

I tossed my head back onto the pillow at the exquisiteness of having him suck and lick my aching flesh. He cupped my other breast in his huge paw-like hand. I didn't have a lot to work with in that department, but he seemed to like it anyway.

When his mouth popped off me, my throat vibrated with a plea for him not to stop, but he only switched to the other breast, sucking me deep and hard against the roof of his mouth. I stabbed my fingers through his dark hair, holding him against me.

He trailed his hands down my sides until his fingertips reached the top of my panties and dipped inside. I held my breath as I tried to focus on what he was doing, but all I could think of was how good he was sucking my nipple. Air touched my wet sex, and I sliced my nails into the skin at the back of his neck as I realized I was now naked in bed with a drop-dead sexy beast of a man.

Lifting his head, he winked at me before kissing his way down the center of my chest. His tongue dipped into my belly button, but he didn't pause on his journey south. Using his shoulders, he spread my legs and settled on his stomach with his face right over my dripping sex.

I bit my lip as I looked down at him, watching as he inhaled deeply, closing his eyes almost as if he were savoring the scent. Heat filled my cheeks, and I was glad I'd had the chance to shave—everything—the night before.

His lips moved, but I couldn't read what he said. And in the next instant, I couldn't have made sense of anything because my brain shut down. Making a V with his index and middle finger of one hand, he spread my folds and touched the tip of his tongue to the little nub hidden there. I fisted my fingers in the covers on either side of me, the pleasure so intense I felt like I was going to fly off the bed and shatter into a million tiny pieces.

Just a few swipes of his tongue and then he was devouring my core. His intimate kiss made me dizzy as the throb deep inside continued to grow out of control. From the vibrations against that little nub, I knew he was groaning or growling. The lack of sound had never been so loud as it was in that moment, when I was desperate to hear the hungry noises that must have been coming from him.

Max touched his hands to the insides of my thighs, spreading me even wider. As I watched, he stabbed his tongue straight into the center of me, and I saw an explosion of bright light right in front of my eyes as the universe crashed down on me.

I didn't know how long it took me to come back to reality, but when I was finally able to open my eyes, it was to find Max on his knees between my thighs, his shorts pushed down over his hips. My mouth went dry at the sight of his perfection.

He was nothing but hard muscle and ink. A light coating of hair trailed down from his navel to the junction at his thighs where his thick cock was straining toward me. I licked my lips as the tip leaked a clear liquid.

Taking one of my hands in his, he guided it to himself and wrapped my fingers around his shaft. My fingers didn't even meet as I held him in my fist, making me feel a combination of nervousness and exhilaration. I was surprised at how hot and soft it was, yet as hard as steel. Tentatively, I stroked upward until my thumb reached the tip and brushed over the drops of sticky liquid dripping from the slit.

My eyes snapped back to his. Almost in a daze, I watched him form the word, "Please."

"I don't know what to do," I confessed.

He grinned. "You have no idea how happy it makes me that I get to teach you, treasure," he signed. "What you are doing is perfect. Do whatever you want to me. I swear, I'll like it all."

Shyly, I got to my knees like he was. Placing my hands on his chest, I gave him a firm shove, and he fell onto his back. His cock stood proudly, and his size became somewhat intimidating. Licking my lips, I tried to wrap my fingers around him once again, but there was a good half-inch gap between my thumb and other fingers.

I had no idea how he was going to fit inside me, but my core clenched at the thought of how far his girth would stretch me. Pressing my thighs together in hopes of containing the renewed ache in my center, I lowered my head until my tongue could swipe over the sticky tip.

He jerked at the first contact, and I shot my eyes to his face. His eyes were clenched shut, and his hands were fisted on either side of him, while his chest lifted and fell in heavy pants. Seeing how such a minuscule touch of my mouth to his most intimate body part caused him to react gave me a sense of power and confidence.

Tightening my grasp, I circled the angry red tip with my tongue before licking down the underside of his cock. The silk-covered steel was so hot to the touch, I wondered if it would burst into flames. When I reached the root, my nose brushed over his balls, and he slapped his hands down on the bed, his fingers clenching in the covers, as if he were aching to reach for me but was forcing himself to let me explore.

Licking back to the tip, I took a deep breath and sucked as much of him as I could into my mouth. When it brushed the back of my throat, I gagged and popped him out of my mouth, gasping for breath. His eyes snapped open, his brow pulled together with concern, but I only smiled and lowered my head again.

This time, I forced my throat to relax and took a little more of him. His entire body began to shake, and I sucked a little harder. My mouth was stretched to the limit, almost to the point of pain. My lips felt swollen as I bobbed my head up and down on him, teaching myself to take more and more of him each time, while both my hands stroked the lower part of his shaft that I couldn't fit into my mouth.

I was having fun, actually enjoying the feel of his tip tickling the back of my throat. I'd discovered that swallowing made his thighs shake, hard, and I loved torturing him with it.

His hands in my hair surprised me. Moving quickly, he

pulled me off his cock and grasped the root, pumping twice before it erupted. Thick ropes of his release landed on his chiseled abs as he sucked in one deep breath after another. When the last drop dripped from the tip, he grasped my hips and pulled me to him, hugging me tight as he tried to catch his breath.

Long minutes passed before he drew back to look down at me. "You are the most amazing treasure. You can't leave me. Not ever."

"I don't want to leave you," I signed. "Just thinking about it hurts, Max."

"Don't worry, baby. I'll kill anyone who tries to take you away." He brushed his lips over mine in a kiss that was so tender, it brought tears to my eyes. I held on to him, never wanting to let go, wanting the kiss to go on forever.

But eventually, we both had to come up for air, and he pressed his forehead to mine. I snuggled closer to him, needing his body heat since I was getting chilled from being naked.

"Let's take a shower," he suggested, getting to his feet. "I need to get us both cleaned up before I make us some break-fast." His gaze went to the clock, and his jaw clenched. "I have to be at work in an hour."

Disappointment hit me hard, but I quickly pushed it down. Of course he had work. I couldn't expect him to hang out with me all day. He had a life outside of me.

He tipped up my chin so my gaze went to his mouth. "It's Saturday, little treasure. I only have to work half a day, and then I'll be right back here to love on you some more."

My heart soared, and I wrapped my arms around his neck. He lifted me, my legs going automatically around his waist as he carried me to the bathroom. With me still wrapped around him, he turned on the shower and let it heat. As it did, he pressed me up against the wall beside the stall door and devoured my mouth.

There were no clothes to block our intimate parts from brushing against each other. His cock was steel-hard again and brushed over my center, making me claw at his back from how exquisite the pleasure was. His chest rumbled from his groan as he opened the shower door and walked inside with me still tangled around him.

I unwrapped my legs from around him and slid down his long, hard body, but he didn't allow me to put more than a few inches between us. Turning me so the spray poured over my head, he grabbed my new bottle of shampoo and lathered my hair. His fingers were thick and magical as he massaged my scalp.

My head fell back on my shoulders, my neck no longer strong enough to hold it up. He grinned at my reaction before massaging down my back all the way to my bottom. Gripping each globe in his hands, he squeezed firmly, causing my center to drip my need down the inside of my thighs.

"So beautiful," he said, his metallic-blue eyes caressing me. "Tell me you're mine, Delaney."

The need to hear someone's voice had never been so strong as it was right then. I ached to hear him say my name. "I'm yours," I mouthed, unsure if he could hear me or not. I didn't speak often, mostly because I didn't have anyone to speak to. It felt almost alien to do it, but I missed it almost as much as I missed my ability to hear.

From the way his eyes began to glitter and his nostrils flared, I suspected he'd heard me and liked the sound of my voice. He stroked the backs of his knuckles over my cheek. "Say my name."

"Max." I gave him what he wanted without question, wanting to please him.

His eyes closed and his chest lifted with a deep inhale, as if he were taking the sound of his name from my lips inside himself and savoring the feeling.

"Little treasure," he started to sign, then paused, his head turning to look at the closed bathroom door. His jaw turned to stone, and his mouth formed a word I didn't understand. Pushing his wet hair back from his brow, he kissed me hard before opening the stall door and grabbing a towel to wrap around himself. "Stay here. I'm going to see who is at the door."

I nodded and watched him go before finishing my shower, missing him even though he was only going to the front door.

By the time I was clean and turned off the water, Max still hadn't returned. I grabbed a towel to wrap around myself and then another for my hair. Opening the door, I peeked out. Not seeing anyone, I tiptoed back to the bedroom and quickly got dressed.

Unsure what to do, I made the bed and then picked up my phone to read one of the free books I'd discovered on the Apple Books app the night before. I got so engrossed in it, I jumped in fright when something brushed my leg.

Max stood over me with a mug of coffee in one hand and a plate of toast and eggs in the other. Grinning, he sat beside me and placed the plate on my lap before taking the phone from my hand and replacing it with the cup of coffee. "Eat," he commanded, and I noticed he was already dressed. He must have come back to the room after seeing who was at the door and then started on breakfast while I was still in the shower. "I have an oil change to do and then a brake job, but that's all I have to do today. It shouldn't take long to get that done, and then I'll be back."

"Who was at the door?" I asked instead of eating like he wanted.

His face became drawn for a moment, but in the next instant, it cleared, and I was left wondering if I'd even seen the anger in his eyes. "Just one of my cousins. He finished cleaning things up for me last night so I could come home and get some sleep since I had to work this morning."

"Oh," I signed, wondering if maybe he'd been mad because his cousin hadn't cleaned up as well as he should have. Deciding to change the subject so he didn't have to think about it, I thanked him for the breakfast. "This is delicious," I praised after the first bite. "You are a great cook."

"I can't do much, but Mom made sure I knew the basics." He bent and brushed his lips over my brow. "I'm going to head down so I can get those two vehicles taken care of. The sooner I'm done, the sooner I can come back and have you all to myself for the next two days."

"I miss you already," I confessed, and his metallic-blue eyes I loved so much darkened.

"Me too, little treasure." With one more kiss, he reluctantly made himself back away. "Eat, and then you can read. I don't want you to be hungry."

It was nice having someone worry if I was getting enough to eat. The experience was so different from what I'd grown used to over the past eight years living at my aunt and uncle's house. Marta fed me when it was time for dinner, and she woke me up with breakfast most mornings, but that had been part of her job. Her kindness was expected.

Not for the first time, I wondered if she'd gotten fired for helping me run away. I hoped not.

"What?" Max was back at my side, tipping my chin up so I was looking at him. "What's wrong? You have this sad, lost look on your face. Tell me what put it there, and I'll fix it."

How could I possibly be falling in love with this guy when I'd only known him a few days? Yet I was falling—

hard—with each passing hour I spent with him. "I was just wondering if something happened to the housekeeper who took care of me at my aunt's house," I told him honestly. "She helped me run away. I hope she didn't get in trouble."

He stroked his fingertips over my cheek before tucking a few locks of my still-damp hair behind my ear. "I'll try to find out for you," he promised.

"Really?" I bit my lip as I contemplated it, then shook my head. "No. I don't want you to go near my aunt and uncle. They're dangerous people. If you got hurt because of me…"

He captured my hands and tucked them against his chest, kissing me and making my protest slip from my mind. "See you soon," he mouthed.

"Bye." I waved.

With a wink, he was out the bedroom door, leaving me to my coffee, breakfast, and the many, many books I'd already downloaded on the app. For the moment, my life was perfect.

I never wanted this to end.

8

MAX

I FINISHED TIGHTENING THE LAST LUG NUT ON THE FINAL TIRE and lowered the car so I could drive it out of the garage bay for the customer whose brakes I'd just changed. I was surprised the guy hadn't wrecked with how badly they had needed changing. There hadn't been anything left of the old pair, which explained the screeching I'd heard earlier when the driver had pulled into the parking lot.

Once I had the car parked to the side so the customer could pick it up, I grabbed my stuff and was ready to make a run for my apartment, desperate to see Delaney again. But before I could even turn for the stairs that would take me back to my little treasure, my sister called my name.

Swallowing a groan, I glanced over to where she had her head sticking out of the shop door. She worked the front a few days a week and on Saturdays when Ben was on duty. Typically, Mom babysat Finn for her most weekends so Lexa and her husband could have some alone time.

"Hey," she greeted when I walked over to her. Her lips were pressed into a firm line. The closer I got, the more I felt her tension. Frowning, I glanced inside the shop. All I saw

65

was the top of the head of the guy whose vehicle I'd just finished working on. We'd started making Saturdays appointment-only to give our other mechanics more time off. This was my Saturday to work, so I was the only person around other than my sister. "The Corolla done?"

"Just finished," I assured her, catching hold of the door so I could step into the shop with her. As I did, the guy sitting in the waiting area lifted his gaze from his phone. His eyes ran disdainfully over me, and I realized this guy didn't live in town, because I had no idea who he was. Figuring he must live in one of the surrounding small towns of Trinity County, I took a moment to memorize the guy's face.

Short ash-brown hair that was thinning on top. Deep-set, light-colored eyes. Broad nose and a slight double chin. With him sitting down, I couldn't tell for sure how tall he was, but I figured my nearly six-foot-tall sister would have at least a few inches on the man.

As I was watching him, he turned his eyes on Lexa, and I felt her stiffen up even more than she already was. He licked his lips as he practically undressed her with his eyes.

I knew my sister could take care of herself. Hell, she was raised by a woman who could handle a gun even better than our MC prez father. Lexa could shoot and wield a blade just as well as any man. On top of that, her husband was the freaking sheriff. But when she was working at the shop, she tried to be polite and courteous. The fact that we were the only garage in the county only had a little to do with the repeat business we continued to have. She was the beautiful, smiling face that kept customers coming back.

Stepping in front of the guy's line of sight and blocking the creep from whatever fantasy he was having of my older sister, I walked over to the counter and pulled up the guy's bill. "Lexa, you go on home," I told her. "I got this."

"I'll wait," she hedged, coming behind the counter with me. "Sir, if you'll just come over so you can pay and sign a few things, you will be on your way in just a few minutes."

He stood and walked over to us. "You still haven't given me your number, pretty thing."

"And I told you, I'm married," she gritted out, her supply of polite and courteous seeming to have been all used up for the day.

"So am I," he said with a predatory grin. With his focus completely on her, he didn't see me ball my hands into fists, ready to clock him in the jaw if he so much as touched Lexa. "What they don't know won't hurt them."

"Her retired marine, sheriff husband might disagree with you," I muttered more to myself than to him, but he still heard me.

His eyes bugged out of his head, and a bead of sweat pebbled on his brow. "You're married to Sheriff Davis?"

"That would be him," I confirmed, forcing my hands to relax so I could get this jerkwad out the door sooner rather than later.

He gulped and produced his wallet from his back pocket. As he pulled out his credit card, I noticed his fingers shaking slightly. "Um, I... Er..." He cleared his throat while I processed his payment. "I was just kidding. Y-you don't need to go telling your man—"

"That you basically propositioned me like I was a hooker?" she finished for him, her tone cold enough to cause frost to form on the windows. Her smile was pure evil as she tossed her hair over her shoulder. The sight of her scar didn't bother me, but up until Ben came into Lexa's life, it was something she'd tried to hide as much as possible. These days, she was more confident in her beauty. "Oh, I already texted him and told him all about your lewd commentary."

I swallowed my laugh as I grabbed the receipt that had printed and handed it to the man. "Your keys are in the center cupholder. Next time, keep a better eye on your brakes. You could have killed someone."

"It's my wife's car," he tried to excuse, snatching the receipt from my hand.

"Even worse," I snapped at him. "A real man doesn't let his woman drive around in a car that could cause her or someone else serious harm."

His face turned red, then purple. When he started sputtering, stumbling over words as he tried to insult me, I leaned forward. "You know who I am, you dickless motherfucker?"

"Some mouthy boy wh-who thinks—" he stuttered, obviously scared of me but still trying to put on a show.

I grinned, glad he didn't know exactly who I was. If he did, he would have already pissed himself. "You're not from around here, are you?"

"He said he moved up this way a few months ago. To be closer to his wife's family," Lexa informed me.

"Ah," I said with a laugh. "And you've already met Ben?"

"When I texted Ben, he said he pulled this guy over earlier in the week because of how loud the brakes were grinding. He was surprised there weren't sparks flying. He wrote him a ticket, but he said he would tear it up once dickless here brought in a receipt for services from us." She smirked up at me when I glanced at her. "That deal is no longer valid. Ben mentioned that he was going to make sure the fine for operating an unsafe vehicle is doubled."

As she was speaking, the sheriff's police cruiser pulled up in front of the shop. The three of us turned our gazes toward the huge window overlooking the parking lot just as Ben stepped out. The look on my brother-in-law's face was murderous.

The customer turned ghostly white, and I snickered as I finished shutting down the computer. "Don't forget to lock up, sis," I told her as I walked toward the back door. "And make sure there's no blood on the floors. You know how Mom hates having to bring in a cleaner." Opening the door, I called over my shoulder, "Let me know if I need to help bury a body."

The bell over the front door jingled as I was going out the back door. Knowing Ben had dickless covered, I jogged up the side stairs to my apartment. Shutting the door behind me, I flipped the locks, not wanting either my sister or brother-in-law to be able to just walk in.

I wanted a little bit longer with my treasure before I had to share her with everyone else.

She wasn't cuddled up on the couch, so I went into the bedroom. When I didn't find her snuggled beneath the covers on our bed, my gut clenched. I'd been so focused on getting my job done, I could have missed her if she'd snuck out. Would she have run off on me?

Just as that nightmarish thought entered my head, I heard a sound from the closet. Frowning, I crossed to it and opened the door. It took a second for my eyes to adjust to the darkness inside the little closet, but when I finally spotted her in the back corner, curled up into a ball, trying to make herself as small as possible, I was ready to destroy whatever had put that fear in her pretty eyes.

Realizing it was me, a pitiful whimper escaped her, and she threw herself into my arms. Feeling how hard she was trembling, I scooped her up and carried her to the bed. Sitting with her in my lap, I held her for a few minutes until some of the tremors stopped before leaning back so I could talk to her.

"What happened?" I signed.

She gulped but quickly answered. "I was looking out the window, trying to see you. I missed you." She lowered her eyes to my chest. "Then I saw the cop's car pull up. I got scared he was here for me."

"You have nothing to fear here, little treasure," I tried to reassure her. "That was just Ben. My brother-in-law. My sister was working in the shop, and he came by to deal with a customer who was being disrespectful to Lexa."

She remained quiet, her chin quivering.

Groaning, I cupped the back of her head and tucked her close. I knew she trusted me, but it seemed it was going to take longer for her to trust that she was safe from all things with me. But I was going to prove to her that nothing could touch her when I was with her.

We sat there for a while, with me rubbing her back in an attempt to soothe us both, before she finally began to relax. When she lifted her head, signing an apology, I captured her hands and lifted them to my mouth so I could kiss each palm. "You have nothing to be sorry for, treasure. Ever."

Twin tears fell down her cheeks. "What if someone takes me away?"

My hold on her hands tightened for a moment before I forced myself to ease my grip. "That won't happen," I promised. "Because I will kill anyone who even tries."

9

DELANEY

READING HADN'T KEPT MY ATTENTION FOR LONG AS EACH minute ticked by without Max there with me. It didn't seem healthy that I missed him to the point of an ache forming in my chest less than ten minutes after he'd left.

Was I being too clingy? Would that annoy him? Some of the girls at school who had boyfriends mentioned that guys hated being smothered. I didn't want to lose Max, so I tried to fight the need to be near him.

But that hadn't stopped me from trying to see him through the window overlooking the front parking lot of the garage. There had been no sign of anyone except for the occasional car driving past until the police cruiser had pulled up in front of the building. As fast as he'd braked, I knew the cop was in a hurry, and when he stepped out, the look on his face told me he wasn't happy.

My only thought was to hide, so I'd grabbed my phone and dived into the closet, trying to make myself as small as possible as I tried to fight the fear of being taken from Max and forced to return to my aunt and uncle.

That fear still hadn't completely faded hours later as Max

sat with me on the couch. The TV was on some movie I hadn't really been paying attention to. The subtitles were on so I could follow along, but my gaze kept going to the closed and locked front door, worried that at any minute it would be forced open and I'd be dragged out of the apartment in handcuffs.

Beside me, Max shifted, pulling his cell phone out of his pocket. When he glanced at the screen, he pressed his lips into a hard line, but he lifted it to his ear. Unlike the night before, he didn't turn his face away as he spoke to whomever was on the other end, so I was able to read some of what he said.

"Don't feel like going out... Dude, I'm exhausted." His jaw tightened before he spoke again. "No, I don't want company either. I'm just going to chill here for the rest of the weekend. See you Monday."

Realizing he was missing out on spending time with someone, I felt guilty that he had to stay home and babysit me. As he dropped the phone on the arm of the couch, I poked him in the arm to get his attention.

"You can go out if you want," I told him. "I'll be fine."

He scowled at me grumpily. "You might be okay, but I wouldn't be. Do you realize how hard it is for me to walk out that door without you—even to go downstairs to work?" He pulled me onto his lap. Lifting my hand, he placed my palm over the center of his chest, letting me feel how hard his heart was pounding. From the erratic way it was beating, I thought maybe he really didn't like being away from me any more than I did being away from him. His throat worked as he swallowed hard a few times before signing again. "I can't fucking breathe when my eyes aren't on you. That might freak you out, but I need you to know what I'm feeling, baby.

This is moving fast. Supersonic fast. But I care about you, treasure."

With my hand still pressed to the center of his chest, I took one of his and placed it in the same spot on my own. After a good ten seconds passed, I signed, "I'm scared of a lot of things, but knowing you care about me is the one thing I can honestly say I don't fear." I gulped, ready to be just as open with him as he was with me. "Because I care about you too."

His metallic-blue eyes darkened with emotion, reminding me of the ocean at night with the moon reflecting in the dark depths. I cupped the side of his face in one hand, my thumb brushing over the stubble on his jaw. He was so beautiful, all I wanted to do was sit there looking at him for hours.

"I'm never letting you go," he signed after a few minutes of just letting me touch him. "You are mine, Delaney." I shook my head, and his face darkened. "Don't say no. I'll make you want to be mine. Just give me a little more time."

I shook my head again, then leaned in and kissed him on the lips—quick—before pulling back. "I don't mean, 'No, I'm not yours.' I mean, 'No, don't call me Delaney.' I like it when you call me 'treasure.' It makes me feel…special."

"Fuck," he mouthed before pressing his forehead to mine. He breathed heavily for a minute before his head snapped up. "I need to warn you, here and now. If you ever try to leave me…" His eyes closed, and he inhaled deeply again, as if the thought caused him physical pain. "Please don't ever leave me, treasure."

I stroked my fingertips over his thick, dark lashes. Leaning in, I touched my lips to each lid. Pulling back, I tilted his chin up, much like he did so often to me, and those eyes I was sure I was already in love with locked with mine. "I will never leave you."

His entire body seemed to vibrate, and I ached to hear the growl that must have been coming from him. I wanted to hear every word, every noise, that left his throat. Just for an hour. That was all I needed, and then I would go back to my silent world without complaining.

But realistically, I knew that wasn't ever going to happen. I was never going to hear anything for the rest of my life. Not even a buzz or ringing in my ears like I'd been told some deaf people heard. I was surrounded by total silence twenty-four hours a day. At first, it had been scary, and then incredibly lonely. Even at school, where I'd been surrounded by peers who had the same disability as I did, I'd felt so alone.

Yet the moment I'd met Max, that loneliness had disappeared.

His hands gripped my backside roughly, and he stood. I wrapped my legs around his waist as soon as he was on his feet, my arms clinging to his shoulders as he sprinted into the bedroom. His incredibly long legs ate up the distance in no time, and before I could fully comprehend where we were going, he was placing me in the center of the bed and following me down.

I held on to the back of his head, pulling his mouth to mine. My body felt like it was on fire, and I needed him to put out the flames before the entire building burned to the ground.

The kiss consumed me, making it impossible to know up from down. When he thrust his tongue into my mouth, giving me a deeper taste of him, the world turned gray around the edges. There was nothing outside the circle of light that surrounded us, and I got lost in the sensations he created with just the brush of his fingertips across my heated flesh.

As if by magic, our clothes disappeared, and soon, I was lying naked beneath him, my lips swollen and tingling, my chest rising and falling as I panted, my thighs coated in arousal. Max leaned over me, his metallic blues eating up the sight of my nakedness as if he were starving. His nostrils flared as he inhaled, and he licked his lips as if whatever he was smelling made his mouth water.

"So beautiful," he mouthed as his head lowered and he licked my left nipple.

The feel of his hot, wet tongue on my hard nub sent little electric shocks through my body to my core, making my clit pulse and throb. The tip of his torturous tongue teased my nipple until I gripped the back of his neck, holding him against me in a silent plea to suck it deep into his mouth.

He did, causing my entire body to shake with how good it felt.

While his mouth was on my nipple, sucking it like he wanted to attach himself permanently to my body, his hands traveled lower. They slid under my bottom, spreading apart my backside and causing the wetness that was already dripping out of my core to flood toward his fingers that were squeezing the flesh in his hands.

My nipple vibrated as he growled then pulled away so he could show the right nipple the same attention. He didn't tease it the way he first did the left. He just sucked the hard little pebble against the roof of his mouth, making my back arch at the intense pleasure and the need to be closer to him.

His groans and growls were nothing more than spine-tingling vibrations against my skin, turning me on more and more. But it became hard to focus on the pleasure he was teasing from my breasts when his fingers started tracing up and down the slit of my backside. It felt so good, yet so naughty. That was a place I never imagined anyone ever touching, not even a doctor, yet suddenly the idea of any part of my body being forbidden to Max seemed ridiculous.

I wanted him to touch every inch of me, including that taboo area. Because even though my cheeks were burning with embarrassment from what he was doing, my core was gushing more and more with how aroused I was from it.

Max's head snapped up, his eyes wild as he mouthed, "Is this too much?"

I bit my lip and shook my head.

Pulling back, he signed, "I need you to say 'Yes' or 'No,' treasure. Can you do that for me?"

Only wanting to please him, I tried to speak the word "Yes." From the way his eyes sparkled, I knew I'd accomplished what he needed from me.

"You're so perfect," he signed. "Now, I need you to tell me if this is moving too fast. If it is, I'll stop." I shook my head vehemently. "I need the word, baby."

"No!"

"Good girl." He stroked one hand down the middle of my chest, coming to a stop right over my belly button. But his hands were so big, they extended all the way to the top of my sex. "If at any time you decide you're not ready for this, all you have to say is 'No,' and I'll stop. No matter how far gone I am, I'll stop."

"Okay," I voiced, but there was no way I was going to tell him no. Not when I was about to turn the bed to ash with how hot he was making me.

10

MAX

SHE WAS SO RESPONSIVE, SO WET, AND ALL MINE.

The little sounds that left her throat were only making it harder to focus on her pleasure when my cock was about to cut a hole through the mattress, it was so hard.

With her verbal consent still ringing in my ears, the melodic sound of her voice like music to my soul, I grasped her luscious ass in both hands and lifted her pussy. Lowering my head, I met it halfway, unable to delay even the milliseconds it would take before I could taste her.

Her whimper of pleasure echoed in the room, and I speared my tongue into her opening. She was so tight, even that was a struggle. As I imagined how hard she was going to squeeze my cock when I finally got inside her, the tip dripped with precome. Her taste exploded on my tongue, forcing a hungry growl from deep in my chest.

Her heels pressed hard into the mattress, and she lifted her lower body harder against my mouth, grinding her clit into my nose as she tried to find relief for the ache I was building deep inside her beautiful body. I could easily pin her to the bed while I ate my fill of her delicious pussy, but I wanted her to take whatever she wanted and needed from me.

"Max!" She got strangled on my name, and my head snapped up just in time to watch her face as she came.

I knew now was the perfect time to put my cock inside her, but I got lost in the beauty of her falling apart for me. Breathing hard, I fisted my cock and shifted up her body. Her legs automatically spread wider for me, even as her entire body continued to shake and convulse from her lingering orgasm.

The tip barely squeezed in, making me curse because the pleasure was crippling, but it was also mixed with a bite of pain that kept me from spilling all over her pussy lips immediately. I realized then and there that this was going to hurt her no matter what I did, and the thought of causing her even an ounce of pain had me stopping, pulling back. No matter that my balls were tight and ready to spill seed at any second. No matter that I'd never been so hard in my fucking life.

I couldn't hurt her.

"No," she sobbed, her hands finding my ass and her nails sinking deep. "No. Please."

I met her tear-filled eyes. "I don't want to hurt you." I tried to explain, but a tear spilled over and she begged me again. "Treasure," I groaned.

"Need you," she whispered, her tears falling faster. "Please."

Fuck, I didn't know what to do. If I thrust into her, I knew I would hurt her physically. But if I didn't make her mine here and now, I'd end up hurting her anyway.

Conflicted, I let her take the decision out of my hands. Gathering her close, I rolled us so she was the one on top of me. Grasping her by the hips, I lifted her until she was straddling me. Delaney looked down at me with an expression of nervous confusion, so I explained. "This way, you can control how much of me you take. You're in charge, treasure."

Her tears dried up, and she smiled down at me. I fisted my cock, holding it so that she could do whatever she wanted with it.

She shifted, positioning her opening right over my tip. I clenched my jaw and told myself to stay perfectly still as her wetness scalded the head of my cock. A few droplets spilled down my shaft, and I prayed for my willpower to hold strong.

Slowly, the tip entered her once again, and she eased down an inch at a time. I watched her face for signs of discomfort or pain. As my girth stretched her, she flinched a little, but that didn't stop her. My little treasure only took more and more, rocking back and forth to work my thickness carefully into her tightness.

Sweat beaded on my forehead and the back of my neck. I still held on to the base of my dick, her pussy not even taking half of me yet, but fuck, she was determined.

My tip hit resistance, and she whimpered for the first time in pain instead of pleasure. I hated that sound. Didn't matter that I was seconds from spilling every drop of come in my balls. Her pained little whines were enough to drive me crazy. I released my cock, ready to grab her and pull her off me. But she must have read my intent in my eyes because she thrust herself down until she was seated to the hilt on my hardness.

"Jesus Christ," I bellowed.

I'd been fucking around since I was fourteen years old. Any girl who wanted to spread her legs for me, I was ready to go. But not a single one of them had ever made me feel this good. Fuck, I couldn't even remember any of their names or faces as Delaney squirmed from side to side, trying to get her body more accustomed to my invasion.

There was only her. I no longer had a past. There was just

this girl, this little treasure I'd been miraculously blessed with. She was my first, because this was the first time I'd ever felt something other than lust.

I wanted Delaney for life.

I'd already known that, but the realization only grew stronger with her virgin blood dripping down my balls while her nails curled into my chest.

The only way I'd ever let this beautiful creature go was when the angel of death dragged my soul deep into the pits of hell.

Sitting upright, I cupped her ass, holding her still so she could adjust to the tree trunk stretching her to the point of pain. I could tell it was hurting her because her brows were pinched together, but there was a brightness in her eyes that I knew was reflected in my own. This feeling of completion was thrumming in my chest, telling me there was nothing in the universe righter than being a physical part of my treasure.

"Are you okay?" I asked, speaking and signing the words.

She gave a tiny nod, but I lifted a brow, and she murmured a small, "Yes," knowing I needed the verbal response.

"You are so beautiful," I told her, pushing her hair back from her face. "You're doing so good, baby. Just breathe through the pain. It will pass."

"You're so big."

My cock liked her words, the stupid bastard thickening even more inside her and causing her to whimper as her delicate, shredded inner flesh protested. I stroked a hand over her perfect ass, trying to soothe her. When my fingers skimmed closer to her back entrance, I felt her clench around me in response, and I knew she liked that.

Fighting a smirk, I did it again, getting the same result. Her whimper this time was a mixture of pain and pleasure, her channel starting to gush with her wetness and ease her death grip on my cock ever so slightly. I kissed her shoulder, then nipped my way up her neck while continuing to tease around her tiny little asshole.

She was too small back there for me to ever try to take her that way. But if my girl liked it, I would buy her any toy she wanted, and I'd play with her for hours if that was what she needed.

"Max," she cried out, burying her face in my neck as she clung to me. Her hips were trying to lift, but she was stretched to the brink, and the small action was difficult for her.

Groaning, I stood and then carefully lowered her to the edge of the bed. I had to drop to my knees so I could stay inside her, and I began to thrust in and out of her at a slow, steady pace.

"No!" she screamed, and I froze, scared I was hurting her.

"Baby—"

"No!" she screamed again. "More. Harder. P-please."

I clenched my eyes closed, knowing if I took her harder, I was going to blow within ten seconds flat. But I couldn't deny her anything.

Pulling back, I sank deep inside her, and she cried out in elation but begged for more. Her cry for more spurred me on, and I gripped her hips, pounding into her until I couldn't see straight, while trying to hold back erupting so she could go over first.

"M-Max," she gasped. "Close."

I stroked my thumb over her clit, and her walls started clenching around my shaft. I saw stars from the pleasure, but that didn't stop me. Throwing my head back, my neck muscles practically spasming as I tried to hold on, I kept pounding her delicate little pussy until she screamed my name.

The sound of my name on her lips mixed with the way her inner walls were rippling around my cock shot me into oblivion, and I exploded deep inside her tight, sweet wonderland.

11

DELANEY

I WAS SURE I LOST CONSCIOUSNESS AT SOME POINT. ONE minute, I was half off the bed, Max still deep inside me. The next, I was lying in the center of the bed, and Max was using a warm washcloth to carefully clean between my legs. His jaw was clenched as he wiped away the smear of blood and the mixture of both our releases, his touch so gentle and caring, I couldn't help falling a little deeper for him.

My eyes wouldn't stay open, no matter how much I willed them to. Letting my lashes lower, knowing there was nowhere in the world safer than right there with Max, I didn't open them again until much, much later.

When reality finally hit me, it was to find myself locked up in the safety of Max's strong arms. His naked body was pressed up against mine, his chest rising and falling as he slept deeply. Yet again, I craved to hear him. The sound of his breathing, to know if he snored, the octaves of his voice when he was happy, mad, sad—and most of all, when he was deep inside me.

I shifted, trying my best not to wake him, but as soon as I moved, he tightened his arms around me and his eyes snapped open. That quickly, he was wide awake. His lips touched my brow before he pushed up onto one elbow so he could lean over me. "How are you feeling?" he signed, his eyes full of concern.

Heat filled my cheeks because I knew he wasn't asking if I was hungry. "I'm okay," I assured him, but my answer didn't seem to ease the frown pulling his brows together. Maybe it was the way I winced when I shifted, the muscles deep in my core tender and a little sore. But the discomfort wasn't anything I couldn't handle. My pain tolerance was higher than most people's, something I'd learned after the explosion that had robbed me of my parents and my ability to hear. "Really."

"I'm sorry." His lips formed the words as he closed his eyes. Inhaling deeply, he snapped them open and he signed, "I hate that I hurt you so badly."

I sat up, a frown of my own lifting my brows. "You didn't hurt me," I tried to tell him, but his gaze dropped to my bare thighs, his jaw clenching so hard, a muscle began to tick there.

Following his gaze, I saw there was a smear of blood on the inside of my thigh, my bare core covered in the same pinkish color. I still had a few more days before my period, so I figured it was from the loss of my virginity.

"Max." I spoke his name, pulling his eyes up to my face —and more importantly, my hands, so I could communicate with him. "I promise, you didn't hurt me. Everything we did…it was amazing. Perfect."

"Treasure," he started, but I pushed him onto his back and straddled his hips. Lowering my head, I pressed my lips to his, ready to prove to him just how unhurt I really was and hopefully make him forget about the little bit of blood.

He caught my hips before I could rub my center over his

steel-hard cock. As if it took no effort at all, he jumped out of bed with me still in his arms and walked out of the bedroom. But not before I saw the red stain on the sheets.

Dang, did all girls bleed that much after their first time?

Then again, Max wasn't exactly small. Not anywhere, and especially not in the cock department. I didn't imagine the girls I'd watched at school talking about having sex had their very first time with the Adonis beast I had.

Using his foot to push open the bathroom door, he crossed to the shower and switched it on.

"We aren't doing that again for a few days," he signed once the water was running and he'd placed me on my feet beside the shower stall door. "Not until I'm sure you have healed."

As gentle and sweet as he'd been, taking such tender care to clean me up after we'd made love, part of me knew he was just looking out for me. But the part of me that was still insecure thought maybe this was just Max trying to tell me he didn't want me now to avoid hurting my feelings.

"If you don't want me, just say so!" I signed angrily.

His eyes narrowed on me. "What did you just say?"

Refusing to repeat myself, I crossed my arms over my chest, not even caring that I was completely naked as I glared up, up, up at him. Dang it, why did he have to be so tall? And so beautiful. Even when he was looking down at me like he wanted to spank me, he took my breath away.

Grabbing my hand firmly in one of his, he guided it to his body, wrapping it around his hardness. My mouth fell open at how hard his silky flesh was. Memories of how amazing he'd felt inside me filled my head, and my inner muscles clenched, causing my channel to burn slightly. "Does that feel like I don't want you?" he demanded, his signs jerky as he shaped each word. "I am throbbing, just as desperate to be inside you right now as I was two hours ago when we made love the first time. I ache for you, treasure." My heart squeezed and my hand tightened around his shaft, but my fingers still wouldn't connect. "I will be this hard for you, want you this bad, when I'm eighty, baby."

I shivered, wanting his words to be true.

Wanting him to want me when he was eighty.

Simply wanting to still be *his* when he was eighty.

"I know you need time to trust me, but you're going to realize I never say anything I don't mean. I tried to warn you." He backed me up against the wall, his head lowering until our gazes were even, but my attention was on his hands as he communicated with me. "You are mine now, treasure. There's no going back. I'm never letting you go. Never."

"I don't want you to let me go."

His nostrils flared, and the sight made my thighs clench together, wetness mixing with the smears of blood coating my skin. "You have no clue what this means. I just hope I don't scare you away before you fully understand."

"There is nothing you could do that will scare me," I promised.

The bathroom was starting to fill with steam, and he scooped me up, carrying me into the shower with him. "Everything I do is to protect you. Even if it's me I have to protect you from."

My nails bit into his shoulders hard, and I shook my head at him. "No," I voiced. "Never you."

"Yes," he signed after placing me on my feet. "Even me. There was so much blood when I cleaned you up after our first time. I spread your thighs and saw how torn you are. We will make love again, but not until you recover from how rough I was earlier."

The self-loathing I saw in his eyes kept me from

arguing with him further. I could see that he was mad at himself, but there was no reason for him to be. I'd asked—begged, actually—for everything he'd done to me. He'd even tried to stop at one point, but I'd wanted him too much. Needed him so desperately, I knew I wouldn't be able to go another minute without him becoming a physical part of my body.

The water rained down on us, but he didn't even seem to notice. "There's something else…"

I frowned when he paused, his hands lifted but not forming words. "What?"

"I didn't use protection." His jaw clenched so hard I feared he was going to break something, but he seemed to force himself to relax. "I need you to know that I've never done that before. I have always worn a condom—"

Something painful filled my chest, and I turned away from him before he could finish signing. I didn't want to think about Max doing to someone else what we'd done. As sweet and gentle as he was, as incredibly beautiful as he was inside and out—of course, he would have been with other girls. Heck, I was surprised he wasn't already in a committed relationship with someone. But it hurt to think about him with anyone but me.

He gripped my waist and turned me to face him, but I couldn't look at him. He said I was his, and more than anything, I wanted him to be mine too. I wanted that even more than I wanted to hear his voice.

"I'm sorry," he signed, his lips forming the words. "I lost my head, and I didn't think about protecting you. I swear, it's the first time it has ever happened, and I will make sure it doesn't happen again."

I gave a stiff nod, unable to fully meet his gaze.

"You have every right to be angry," he continued. "Just

understand that, no matter what happens, I'm in this one hundred percent."

I didn't even know how to respond to that, so I only nodded again. I wasn't worried about the no-protection thing. Even though no one had ever sat me down and had the whole birds and bees talk with me, I'd taken health and science classes in school. I knew I was at a safe point in my cycle when I didn't have to worry about getting pregnant.

"Treasure, tell me you don't hate me."

"I don't," I signed, keeping my eyes on his hands and not his face, trying to hide my pain from him.

But stupidly, a tear spilled down my cheek.

"There's no need to be scared…" he began.

"I'm not scared," I replied before turning my back on him again. I reached for my shampoo and started to lather my hair, trying desperately to get my emotions under control. I should have felt shy, standing in the shower with him, naked and wet. But there was none of that. All I could think about was him with a long line of other girls. Maybe in this same shower, in that same bed where he'd claimed me.

The pain made it impossible to breathe, and I dropped my hands from my hair, wrapping my arms around my middle in an attempt to keep the hurt away.

Max jerked me around to face him. "Tell me what's wrong," he commanded, his eyes wild. "What did I do?"

"Nothing." I tried to evade, but he wasn't having it.

"Delaney." I flinched when he signed my name. I didn't want to be "Delaney" to him. I only wanted to be his "treasure." "Baby, tell me so I can fix it."

"I want to be the only one," I finally explained, but he pulled his brows together in confusion.

"Only what?"

"Everything," I told him honestly. "The only one you've kissed, touched, held… Been inside of."

Understanding filled his metallic-blue eyes, and his chest expanded as he inhaled deeply. "I want that too, treasure. I'm so sorry that I didn't wait for you. If I had known I would find you one day, I swear to you, I would have waited."

His answer surprised me. "Really?"

Max cupped my chin in his hand, forcing me to focus on his mouth. "Really," he spoke the word before signing, "In my heart, you *are* the only one. Because this is the first time I've ever felt like this."

The pain that had made it nearly impossible to breathe only moments before eased, and I melted against him. "Max…"

"You need to understand that there is nothing to be jealous of," he signed, his eyes dancing over my face. "I'm yours, treasure."

12

MAX

After spending the entire weekend locked in the apartment with Delaney cuddled on top of me, I was not in the mood to get up for work Monday. But I knew if I didn't get my ass out the door, one of my parents would come looking for me.

Promising myself I would introduce my treasure to both of them soon, I kissed my girl goodbye, tucked the covers up around her, and then forced myself out the door. Thankfully, the day was busy, with one customer after another, and I only paused to text Delaney to make sure she had eaten breakfast. At lunch, I had to take care of something for Uncle Trigger, so I sent another text, telling her to eat without me and I would see her after I took Nova home from school at the end of the day.

Both times, I got a text back assuring me that she was fine and that she'd eaten. She was spending the day reading on her phone, so she was content to stay snuggled on the couch. But she missed me.

Fuck, I loved getting messages like that from her. It made me feel a little less sick in the head for how much I ached

90

from missing her. If she missed me even after I'd spent the entire weekend smothering her with my presence, then she wouldn't freak out that I had trouble breathing just being in the garage below her all day.

I did my time at the middle school with Reid, who spent the few minutes before the bell rang ragging on me for bailing on him all weekend.

"Your dick broke or something?" my cousin and best friend grumbled as I just sat on my bike. "You never turn down the chance to go to one of the sorority parties on campus and hook up with one of those spoiled little rich girls at Trinity."

He was right. Before my treasure, I would have been all too happy to spend the entire weekend finding a different girl to get my dick wet with. But that shit was over. Knowing he wasn't going to drop it until I at least gave him something, I shrugged. "I met someone."

Reid barked out a laugh. "Yeah, okay."

"No, man. Seriously." I pulled out my phone and showed him one of the many pictures I'd snapped of Delaney over the weekend. It was one where she'd been curled up beside me on the couch. Her focus was on the book she was reading on her phone while I'd watched TV. She had one arm draped over my stomach, her head on my chest. All you could see in the picture was the side of her beautiful face, but it was all I was going to let him see of her for now. "This is my girl."

Reid's eyes nearly popped out of his head as he looked at her. "Holy shit. Do your folks know?"

I shook my head, pocketing my phone once again. "I'm waiting. Giving her time to get used to my shit before I scare her with Mom and Dad."

He snorted. "You're more intense than either Aunt Raven or Uncle Bash, brother."

I grinned. "True. But my little treasure likes me anyway."

Reid coughed on his next laugh. "Damn, man. You're already gone for this chick."

I wasn't even about to deny it. He was right. I was gone for Delaney, and I never wanted to find my way back. "I need to get myself an SUV or a truck. I love having that girl on the back of my bike, but I don't want her to get sick when it rains or snows in the winter."

"For fuck's sake." He shook his head at me, his amusement fading. "I'm losing you to the dark side of a relationship. Who am I going to get to be my wingman?"

"Jack. Kingston. Chance. Elias." I started listing names as the bell rang, making him grumble in mock despair. Most of the time, my four cousins were already at the sorority parties before we even showed up. Getting any of them to be his wingman wasn't going to be a problem, especially his younger brother.

"I know a guy two towns over," Reid said just as I spotted Nova coming our way. "I did some private construction for him on his home office a while back, off the books. He owns a dealership. Said if I was ever shopping for a cage, he'd throw me a good deal. Let me make a call, and I'll go with you tomorrow to check out what he has available."

"Yeah, thanks, man." If I got the vehicle sooner rather than later, I could take my girl shopping Friday evening. Satisfied with that plan, I helped Nova onto the back of my bike. "How was your day, runt?"

She glowered at me at the hated nickname. "I'm glad this is the last week of school. I'm so ready to go to New York for the summer."

"Vitucci flying in for Garret and River's graduation this weekend?" Reid asked curiously.

Her green eyes brightened. "He's supposed to be here

Saturday morning. Uncle Ciro and Aunt Scarlett as well. Maybe some of their kids."

"Tavia and Theo are coming too," I informed Reid, knowing from my mom's excitement earlier in the day that my adopted sister would be coming with her husband and baby daughter for the weekend. Mom had seen them just a few weeks before at River's birthday party, but when it came to the girl she considered her second daughter, she was always happy to spend as much time as possible with Tavia and baby Rai.

Since the whole family would be present, I figured introducing Delaney at the graduation party Saturday afternoon would work the best. What I really wanted to do was keep my treasure all to myself for a little more time, but I didn't know if I could keep her a secret from my mom for much longer. I knew Delaney was the girl I was going to spend the rest of my life with, and I wanted Mom to know it too.

With the last parent driving out of the parking lot, I started my bike and tipped my chin at my older cousin. "Text me later when you talk to your guy."

Reid nodded. "I'll let you know, brother."

--

As soon as I walked through the front door, Delaney jumped up off the couch and threw herself into my arms. I caught her around the waist, her short legs going around my hips as she jerked my head down and kissed me.

Groaning, I had enough sense to flip the locks before I carried her over to the couch and dropped down with her in my lap, never once breaking our heated kiss. Her soft hands pushed my cut off my shoulders and then started on the buttons of my work shirt.

Knowing where this was going, I ended the kiss, but she only attached her mouth to my neck, sucking on my pulse and driving me out of my fucking mind. My hands bit into her sweet ass, knowing I needed to stop this. She hadn't complained once about being in pain, not by so much as a grimace since Saturday evening. But even though my cock was constantly steel-hard just thinking about her, I'd fought the need to take her again and again all weekend.

The memory of how much blood there had been after we'd made love that first time, how red and torn she'd been when I'd cleaned her up, made it easier. I'd lost control and hurt her once, and I'd be damned if I would do it a second time.

Delaney got my shirt half unbuttoned before she gave a frustrated cry and attached her mouth to my left pec.

Breathing hard, I caught the back of her head and made myself lift her head. "Be honest with me," I signed, my cock pulsing against her pussy through the confines of my boxers, jeans, and her panties. I was only just realizing she was in nothing but one of my T-shirts and a pair of bikini briefs. "Are you hurting?"

She shook her head vehemently, raking her nails down my chest, trying her best to distract me. When one of her nails scratched over a nipple, I had to lock my jaw in an attempt to keep from fucking her then and there.

"I mean it, treasure. I want to know if you feel even a little discomfort."

Again, I got a shake of her head in response.

Seeing that I meant business, she stood and pushed her panties over her hips. Straightening, she took my left hand in hers and then guided it to her pussy. When she pressed two of my fingers inside her, we both released tortured groans. She was soaked and so fucking tight, I nearly exploded in my boxer briefs.

And as I slowly stroked my fingers in and out of her, she

didn't flinch or whine in pain. She closed her eyes, her head falling back on her shoulders as she whispered my name. I eased a little deeper, trying to feel if there was anything torn, but I felt nothing that would tell me I might hurt her when I took her this time.

Cursing because I was so damn weak, I grabbed her hips and dropped onto my back, pulling her over my face as I lay down. Her little cries were pure torture as I ate her dripping pussy until she was trembling against my face.

Holding her steady with one hand, I unfastened my belt and quickly freed my cock from its confines before lifting her off my mouth and positioning her over the tip.

But before I could thrust up into her molten sweetness, I remembered the need for protection.

"Sonofabitch," I bellowed. If I kept this shit up, my treasure was going to make me a daddy before either of us was ready. It wasn't that I didn't want kids. Hell, I'd give her as many as she asked for. But I wanted some time with just her and me for a good bit before we started making babies.

I rolled us so she was under me and then jumped to my feet. "Be right back," I signed before running into the bedroom to grab two condoms out of the closet. I'd never brought anyone back to the apartment when I would hook up in the past, so I didn't keep them in the bedside drawer.

I tore one open and started sheathing my cock before I even got back to the couch. She lay there, watching me with a sexy little smile teasing at her lips while her eyes stayed glued to what my hands were doing.

Sliding between her legs again, I lifted one and bent it back toward her chest as I thrust deep into her tight haven.

"Sweet Jesus," I groaned. She was just as tight as she had been the first time, but there was no resistance now. Her walls clenched around me, already milking me toward a powerful explosion. Rolling my hips back, I began thrusting in and out of her.

"Max!" she screamed my name, revving me up higher and higher. "Please."

Licking my thumb, I pushed my hand between us and rubbed her hard clit in tight little circles, causing her to whimper beneath me. A half-dozen more pumps of my hips and she detonated, taking me with her.

Out of breath, I dropped down onto her, kissing every inch of her face.

When I lifted off her, the first thing I asked was if she was okay.

She gave me a sleepy smile. "Perfect," she mumbled, her lashes already lowering.

While she slept, I got rid of the condom and then came back to take care of her. Carrying her to our bed, I tucked her in before taking a shower. She was still sleeping when I walked back into the bedroom with a towel wrapped around my hips. It was getting late, and I still needed to feed her dinner.

In the kitchen, I looked through the pantry for something that might tempt her, but all I found were some packs of ramen and a few cans of beef stew. Shaking my head at how pathetic the cabinets were stocked, I called in an order to Aggie's and got ready to pick it up. Mom and Aunt Flick had been on me about them bringing over food, but I'd kept putting them off, saying I was too busy.

Half an hour later, I walked into Aggie's, only to find my sister standing at the counter with Finn toddling around at her feet.

Seeing me, my nephew screamed and threw himself against my legs. Laughing, I bent to pick him up. There were some features the kid shared with his dad, but for the most part, Finn looked like Lexa, which meant he looked a lot more like me than he did Ben.

Lifting him high, I blew raspberries on his stomach, making him giggle and cling to my head until I lowered him. Keeping him in one arm, I turned to face my sister. She stood there waiting for her food, grinning at me and her son.

"Perfect timing," she said. "I was just picking up dinner."

"Me too." I shifted Finn in my arms. "Ben working late tonight?"

"Nah, he will probably beat me home. I was going to call you later. I ordered River a present for her graduation, and it's supposed to be in by Friday. But it's being delivered to the store and not my house. Do you think you could pick it up at the mall for me Friday evening? Ben will be working late then, and I hate driving all that way alone with Finn."

"No problem." I was taking Delaney to the mall Friday anyway, so it wasn't going to be out of the way for me. Not that I told my sister that. If she found out about my girl, she would go running to Mom. Those two never kept secrets from each other, which was sweet, but also a pain in the ass when I needed Lexa to keep her mouth shut about shit.

"Great. Thanks, baby brother." She kissed my cheek then took her son from my arms as the waitress brought out a bag of to-go boxes.

I waited until she was out the door before paying the girl for my own food order. But instead of her going into the back to grab my stuff, Kingston brought it out. "You must be starving if you ordered this much food," my cousin said with a sly grin as he handed over the two bags. "Either that, or you got company."

"I'm hungry," I said with a shrug. "You make sure there were extra tomatoes and pickles on that burger?"

He nodded, but his brows went up. "Yeah, but since when do you eat anything but cheese and meat on your burger?"

"Since now," I growled, grabbing the bags. "See ya, man."

By the time I plated our food and carried it into our bedroom, she was already waking up. Seeing me with dinner, she sat up with a bright smile on her face that could have lit up the room all on its own.

"Hungry, treasure?" She nodded, and I placed the plate on her lap. She loved Aggie's cheeseburgers, and she seemed to have a thing for tomatoes and pickles on them. To me, vegetables made a burger not worth eating, but she gobbled that shit up and licked her lips when she was done.

I watched her tongue swipe over that full lower lip and knew it was going to be a long night.

Putting our plates on the nightstand, I pulled her onto my lap, all too happy to get zero sleep if it meant I got to gorge on her for dessert.

13

DELANEY

I COULDN'T HELP STARING WIDE-EYED AS WE WALKED HAND in hand. The last time I'd been in a mall was right before my parents had taken me on our last family vacation. Mom and I had gone shopping for the trip while Dad was at work. Even though I was an only child, Mom never let me feel lonely. We had girls' days several times a month when we went shopping, got our nails done, or just went to a movie together.

But it had been over eight years since I last was around so many people outside of school. If I needed clothes, Marta would buy them for me and then hang them in my closet while I was in class. But unless I absolutely had to have something for school or I outgrew something, new clothes had been a luxury I was rarely given.

"Where to first?" Max asked as we stood in front of the mall directory on the first floor. "I have to stop at this store before we leave to grab something Lexa ordered for our cousin River, but other than that, we can go anywhere you want."

A few of the stores listed on the directory I knew, but a

good portion of them were new to me. Biting my lip, I shrugged, feeling embarrassed that I had no idea what kind of merchandise most of the stores even sold.

Max brushed the backs of his fingers over my cheek before signing, "How about we just walk around first, and if anything catches your eye, we can go in and have a look?"

I nodded, and he took my hand. The first stop we made was at the pretzel shop, where he grabbed two cinnamon-sugar pretzels and a large soft drink for us to share. I devoured mine as we took the escalator to the top floor.

The shops all had pretty things in their windows, but they looked expensive and I didn't want to take advantage of Max when he'd already been so generous with me. But as we started on the second floor, Max began to get cranky because I hadn't stopped at any of the stores yet.

"What about this place?" he asked outside a store that had several dresses and other summer outfits on their mannequins in the front window. "That dress would look hot on you, baby. And you need something pretty to wear to the wedding tomorrow."

I frowned up at him. "What wedding?" I signed in a rush, my heart already pounding against my ribs with nervousness.

He shrugged like he hadn't just dropped a huge bomb in my lap. "My cousin is getting married after her graduation tomorrow. It's a big surprise for her that her boyfriend is throwing together with her parents."

"You want me to go with you?"

"Of course, treasure." He tugged me into the store. "I know I've been keeping you all to myself this week, but it's time to introduce you to my family. Since everyone will be there tomorrow, this is the perfect opportunity."

Now that I knew I was going to be meeting his family, the

people who meant so much to him, I had to find the perfect outfit. I didn't want his mom to see me for the first time and think I was a slob.

"Get whatever you want," Max urged when I glanced at the price tag of a dress I thought might be suitable for a wedding. Having never actually attended one before, I didn't really know what to wear to it, but the dress was a mixture of sweet and elegant.

"It's too much," I tried to argue, hating that he was spending so much money on me.

He grabbed the dress I'd just placed back on the rack and took my hand, leading me back to the dressing rooms. Someone was just leaving one of the stalls, and he pushed me into it, thrust the dress against my chest, and commanded me to try it on before closing the door in my face before I could argue.

Mutinously, I took my time changing. The dress hit me mid-thigh, the top clung to my chest, emphasized my small waist, and then flared out at the hips with the help of a little tulle. I loved how it looked on me, but it was so expensive…

The vibrations on the door told me someone was knocking, and I knew my time was up. Reluctantly, I opened the door, ready to tell Max I didn't like the dress.

His reaction, however, gave me pause. The way his metallic eyes widened, his nostrils flared, and his mouth dropped open, I knew he liked the dress on me even more than I did. Given the tent in his jeans, there was no mistaking he enjoyed seeing me in something so beautiful.

My period had started on Tuesday, just as I'd expected it to, so we hadn't had sex since Monday. But by tomorrow, I would be off my period, and I was going to jump him again as soon as I possibly could.

Swallowing hard, he ran a hand down his face, and I wondered if he was groaning. "You're getting it," he signed after another few moments of just standing there looking at me. "I'll probably end up killing someone tomorrow, but burying a body will be worth it if I get to look at you in that all night."

I grinned. He was joking about killing people. It was kind of adorable. My sweet Max was a gentle giant. He wouldn't hurt a fly. It was one of so many things that I loved about him.

"Fine," I gave in. "But only because I like the way you're looking at me right now."

"Shoes," he said, pointing over his shoulder. "Nothing with a tall heel. I don't want you to hurt yourself."

"You are so bossy," I complained, hiding my lingering smile as I walked past him in search of a pair of flats. He didn't need to worry, I'd never even been given the chance to wear shoes with a high heel to them, so I wasn't going to embarrass myself by trying the first time I met his parents and risk face-planting right in front of them.

I found a pair of black ballet slippers that I figured would go with anything, and I tried them on. When Max gave me a thumbs-up in approval, I went back to the dressing room to change back into the jeans and T-shirt I'd been wearing.

Of course, he wasn't done spoiling me, though. We didn't leave the store until there were a few more outfits added to the pile. Then he was pulling me into Victoria's Secret for a few pretty bras, some sexy panties, and even a hoodie and some sweats in my size. I didn't complain about how much he spent in that particular store because it seemed like the more intimate items were just as much for him as they were for me.

Afterward, we walked around a little more, but outside

the bookstore, I paused when I caught sight of a figure in the window. Whipping my head around, I looked to where I thought I'd seen a familiar face. But by the time I turned my head, the person was gone, a small group of teenagers in his place.

My heart was pounding against my ribs, but I tried to tell myself I was seeing things. It wasn't likely that my uncle's second-in-command, of all people, would be walking around window-shopping at the mall. I kept telling myself that, and when I didn't see him again, I pushed it completely from my mind.

If I thought our shopping adventure was over, however, I was mistaken. After we picked up the package for his sister on the first floor of the mall, he guided me into a jewelry store.

"No, Max." I glared up at him. "This is too much."

"Hush," he commanded and dropped the many bags in his hands as a woman dressed in a black skirt and red top walked over to us with a bright smile on her face.

"How can I help you today?" she asked, her gaze bouncing from Max to me expectantly.

"Earrings, necklaces, bracelets. Whatever she wants," he told her as he signed the words so I could understand since he was facing her and not me.

Her eyes lit up even more. "Of course," I read her lips. "Let me show you a few of the pieces we just got in."

As she walked over to a case a little farther away, Max started to follow her, but I stayed where I was. When he realized I wasn't beside him, he turned back and took my hand in his, pulling me over to where the sales rep was already removing several pieces of beautiful jewelry from the case she was standing behind.

"This set will go nicely with your dress for tomorrow," he

observed, taking the necklace from the woman's hand and holding it up to my neck.

"Lovely," she agreed. I glared at her, but she only winked.

He took the earrings next, holding one to my ear and nodding. "Beautiful." His mouth formed the word, his eyes glittering hungrily down at me.

Turning back to the woman, he said something, but I couldn't read his lips and he wasn't signing so I could know what he was saying. She nodded and moved over a few cases before coming back with two more pairs of earrings. He pointed to the pair of diamond hoops.

I tried to protest again, but he ignored me, buying the necklace and earring set as well as the hoops. Max gave her his credit card, and she started boxing up the jewelry. I didn't even see the prices of the items, but I knew each one of them must have been expensive. I didn't like him spending so much money on me.

Less than two weeks ago, I was homeless. My meals had been out of dumpsters, and I'd smelled just as horrible as the trash I picked through in hopes of finding something edible. Now, this guy was spoiling me with new clothes and diamonds.

But what could I possibly give him in return? He was so amazing and kind, and I had nothing to repay him with.

Swallowing the lump that filled my throat, I turned away as the woman placed the boxes in a fancy bag with cloth handles. Max took it, grabbed the other bags, then guided me out of the store, and thankfully, the mall itself.

I felt his gaze on the top of my head, but I kept mine trained on the ground as we walked through the parking lot to where he'd parked his brand-new Tahoe. Tuesday, he'd come home from work, showered, and then left after promising to bring home dinner. When he returned, he had the Tahoe he kept saying was now ours.

I didn't understand how it could belong to both of us. I didn't even have a driver's license. Heck, I didn't even have a diploma. I had been only months away from graduating when Marta urged me to run away.

Realizing just how useless and pathetic I really was, tears filled my eyes, but I tried to blink them back.

The liftgate of the SUV rose with a press of a button on Max's key fob, and he placed all the packages in the back. The press of another button had the trunk lowering on its own, and he scooped me up, carrying me to the passenger side, where he placed me in the seat and then made me look at him.

"Are you angry with me?" he asked, his eyes troubled.

I shook my head. How could I possibly be angry with him when he'd just spent the last few hours spoiling me?

He turned me in the seat, spread my legs, and stepped between them. He had to practically bend in half, but he put his face close to mine. "I don't like it when you are upset. Talk to me, treasure. Tell me what I did wrong, so I can fix it."

"All you do is spend money on me," I exploded, my hands shaking as I signed each word.

He caught my hands, his beautiful face turning stormy. "I enjoy spoiling you, baby. Seeing you in pretty things that I know I bought for you makes me happy."

"People are going to think I'm only with you for your money."

Max shrugged. "Who cares what other people think? The only person's opinion that matters to me is yours." He skimmed his lips over mine, making my brain shut down at the first contact. My arms went around his shoulders, holding him closer, wanting to deepen the kiss. But he pulled back without giving me what I wanted. "I'm going to be honest with you, okay?" He waited for me to nod before continuing. "I'm not a millionaire, but I have saved up my money, and I can take care of us without having to worry about paying bills or keeping food on the table."

"That wasn't what I was worried about," I was quick to tell him.

"Then what, baby?" he implored. "Tell me what has that look in your eyes so I can erase it."

I lowered my gaze to my lap. "I'm worthless," I signed. "I will never be able to pay you back for all the things you buy me."

He didn't move for the longest time, and eventually, I gathered my courage to look up at him. I'd never really seen Max angry before, but suddenly, he looked livid. "Don't ever call yourself worthless again, treasure."

"But I am."

He balled his hands into fists. "Are you blind as well as deaf?" he signed.

Hurt filled my chest, and a tear spilled down my cheek.

He shook his head, his eyes like fire as they skimmed over me. "You are the most amazing creature I have ever met. No one has even come close to touching the parts of my heart you already have. How can you not see that you are priceless?"

"Max."

He moved in closer. "I don't want you to speak about paying me back for anything ever again. What part of 'mine' did you not understand? We belong to each other now, baby. That means what's mine is yours."

"But I have nothing to offer you." I tried to make him

understand. It was important to me that I be able to give him something in return for all that he was giving me.

He pressed one hand to the center of my chest, his amazing eyes capturing mine for nearly a full minute before he signed the words that sent me over the edge, free-falling. And I knew, without a shadow of a doubt, that I loved him. "You have this, treasure, and that is all I will ever want."

14

———

DELANEY

Max didn't have to work Saturday morning, but he had to go to his cousins' graduation. He wanted me to go with him, but I wasn't sure if it was the right time to drop our relationship in his family's lap.

After it was over, he came home, bringing Nova with him. When he'd asked if I needed things to do my hair with, I'd admitted I had no idea how to style my hair except to put it in a ponytail or to do the occasional simple braid. There had been no one to teach me about curling irons or any of the other tools.

I was happy to see Nova, and when she announced she was there to help me get ready for the wedding, I nearly cried. We spent over an hour in the bathroom while she—a thirteen-year-old—taught me how to use the curling iron she said I could have. When my hair was all curly and shiny, she gave me a quick tutorial on makeup. We kept it simple with foundation, a little eye shadow, mascara, a touch of blush, and some lip gloss.

But when it was time for the wedding, I urged Max and Nova to go without me. From what the two of them told me about their cousin River and her boyfriend Maverick, it seemed like things were already going to be dramatic enough without adding me to the mix.

Max wasn't happy, but Nova agreed with me and convinced him to let me stay. As soon as it was over, he was back at the apartment, ready to drag me to the reception if I didn't agree to go with him.

I was already waiting at the window, watching for him. He'd taken his motorcycle to the wedding, but when he came back for me, it was the Tahoe that he picked me up and placed me inside.

As soon as my seat belt was on, I pulled down the visor to check my reflection in the mirror. I was so nervous to meet his family that I was shaking, but he only took my hand in his much larger one and placed it on his thick thigh as he drove.

The parking lot of Hannigans' bar was overflowing with vehicles and more motorcycles than I'd ever seen in one place in my life. My heart started racing as he got out and came around to help me out. Once my feet were on the ground, I tugged on my dress. It had seemed so perfect when I tried it on at the store the day before, but now that I was only minutes away from meeting his mother, it suddenly seemed too short.

Moms didn't like it when their sons dated girls who dressed too sexy, right?

Dang it, I wasn't sure.

I wanted his mom to like me. Wanted her to accept me so that Max would be happy and wouldn't second-guess our relationship.

Before we reached the door to the bar, he turned to face me. His gaze skimmed over me, darkening with appreciation. "You look beautiful," he told me. "Don't worry. Everyone is going to love you."

I bit my lip and nodded, hoping he was right. Opening the door, he guided me in with a hand on my hip. As soon as we were inside, he took my hand, holding it possessively while I glanced around at all the people. Off to one side was a table with a huge wedding cake. A buffet of food was set up along another wall. Tables were pushed together in one area where people were sitting around, eating, their mouths moving, and they were laughing.

On the dance floor, a beautiful blond girl in a wedding dress was dancing with a man in an Angel's Halo MC cut like the one Max was wearing. There were a lot of guys in the same leather vests out there dancing, some of them looking like fathers with their daughters. Others seemed younger and danced with women I could only assume were their mothers.

Since I was taking in all the people, it took me a moment to realize that everyone's attention was slowly being directed at me. Beside me, I could feel Max tensing up, and I noticed he was glaring at everyone.

Oh no, had I already done something wrong?

I tugged at my dress, sure that I wasn't dressed right or that my makeup made me look silly. I tried to tug my hand free of his grip, but he only tightened his hold for a moment before he dropped it so he could speak to me. "You look beautiful," he said again, but his smile was tight.

"Why are you mad?" I asked, glancing around again quickly.

His face softened ever so slightly. "I'm not mad, treasure. I just don't like that all these assholes are looking at you like they want to snatch you away from me."

I lifted my hand to touch his chest. "I'm yours," I reminded him, and I was rewarded with his nostrils flaring in pleasure.

"Let me introduce you to Mom, and then we can eat, okay?"

I gave a small smile, nodding, but my pulse escalated. This was it. I was about to come face-to-face with his mother.

Please, please, please let her like me.

When we turned around, I swear an older version of Nova stood in front of us. With her long blond hair and intelligent green eyes, she put off an aura of…power. All she did was stand there, her eyes going from Max to me, the wheels in her brain openly turning as she took in the way her son was holding my hand.

His thumb rubbed soothingly over the inside of my wrist before he released me so he could sign while he spoke to the beautiful woman standing before us. "Mom, this is Delaney."

He paused, and I watched as his head shifted, his eyes turning glacial as he glared from one guy in an MC cut to another before focusing back on me. My heart gave a huge leap in my chest when the blue turned back to that metallic color I loved so much. "And she is mine," he signed, claiming me in front of everyone who could read his words as well as hear them.

My body suddenly felt as if it were being engulfed in flames, and all I wanted to do was climb him like a tree and kiss him.

But then I realized where we were and who was in front of us, and I felt my face heat. Raven was looking at me like a bug under a microscope, her eyes assessing me as if she couldn't understand what she was seeing.

Crap, crap, crap. Could she tell I was having naughty thoughts about her son?

She just stood there. Not speaking, not even trying to sign a greeting. Max told me that his mom was the one to first teach him ASL, so I knew she would at least know how to tell me "Hi." The longer she didn't move, only continued to look at me like I didn't belong there, the more my chest began to tighten.

And then she shifted, giving me her back. I was so discouraged and hurt by the action that it took me a moment to realize she was using her body as a shield against the woman who was marching toward us with her eyes blazing.

I stepped closer to Max, who put his hand at my waist and tucked me against him as he said something, but he wasn't signing and his mouth was moving too quickly for me to understand what he was saying. Around us, others were stepping toward us, as if they were enjoying the show we were putting on for them, or maybe they wanted me to leave.

Maybe they knew I was homeless, and they didn't like that I was with Max. He was so sweet, so kind, and they probably thought I was taking advantage of him. It wasn't true, but I would understand if they didn't believe it.

Pressed so close to Max, I could feel the vibrations in his chest and knew he was shouting. That only made me feel worse, and tears began to sting my eyes. I pressed my face into his side, trying to hide them.

A small, soft hand on my arm made me jerk. Curious, I lifted my head enough to see who was touching me and found Nova standing there with a reassuring smile on her beautiful face.

"It's okay," she signed. "It isn't what you think."

I frowned at her. "They hate me," I signed back, and she started shaking her head before I'd even finished.

Max was still vibrating, his mouth moving fast, making it impossible to make out a single word. I glanced at his mom, still standing like a human shield between us and the woman in the pretty dress who seemed both angry and desperate to get to me. From how red her face was and how quickly her lips moved, I thought maybe she was shouting too.

The blonde in the wedding dress appeared beside the screaming woman, tears in her eyes as she tried to help Raven, tugging on the brunette's arm in an attempt to pull her back. The man she'd been dancing with stood off to the side, not helping, just watching with wide eyes, and I wanted to know what everyone was saying.

The bride was crying, and it was all my fault.

Not wanting to ruin the wedding reception any more than I already had, I jerked out of Max's hold, ready to make a run for the door. But before I could take more than a step, someone blocked my path. I looked up into a pair of brown eyes and gulped. He wasn't as tall as Max, nor as wide, but there was something about this guy that made me take a step back.

Max was beautiful, but this guy…he was something else entirely. I didn't know if I wanted to stop and just take in everything about him, or run as far and as fast as possible in the opposite direction.

He screamed danger, but I wasn't sure if that danger was good for me or not.

Nova moved so that she was standing between us, her smile still soft and reassuring. "This is Ryan. Don't worry, he's harmless. For the moment…" My eyes widened at her introduction. She had told me all about her "best friend," and now I understood their relationship a little more…yet I was beyond confused.

When she'd told me about Ryan, I'd pictured a guy not much older than she was. Admittedly, five years wasn't much of an age gap at all, but with Nova thirteen and him almost nineteen, that gap looked more like the Grand Canyon. I got the feeling Nova might be crushing on Ryan, but as I watched

Ryan look down at her, there was no heat in his eyes, only what seemed like pure adoration.

Max's comment about Ryan imprinting on Nova at first sight came back to me, joking about the *Twilight* books and how Jacob had imprinted on Bella's daughter. I could see exactly what he meant by it now, and I decided to trust Nova's Ryan.

"I just want to leave," I signed. "I'm ruining this for River."

Nova glanced over my shoulder then up at Ryan. The two of them seemed to have a telepathic conversation before he shrugged and she stepped forward. "Max will kill me if I let you leave," she signed. "But let's get you out of the line of fire."

She guided me away from Max and toward where the tables were set up. Ryan pulled out two chairs, and Nova urged me down in one as she took the other. I glanced around, noticing that people were practically giving themselves whiplash from how they kept looking from me to where Max was still yelling at the woman on the other side of his mother.

Ryan positioned himself in front of me, making it impossible for anyone to see me and effectively forcing the others to stop trying to look at me.

"Your aunt hates me," I told Nova, my shoulders drooping as I sat back in my chair.

"No, she doesn't," Nova dismissed. "I think she was just surprised. And then Aunt Kelli started getting hysterical—which, by the way, never happens—and things became a little clearer."

Her answer only confused me more. "Who is Kelli?"

"You know, the crying crazy woman Aunt Raven was holding back. Trust me, if Aunt Raven didn't already like you, she wouldn't have gotten in the way of that hurricane."

Someone in a dark suit placed two glasses of something fizzy in front of us, but before I could get a look at their face or even tell them "thank you," they were gone. Nova picked up her drink and took a sip, and I did the same. The lemon-lime soda felt good on my throat, and I took another thirsty swallow before putting the glass back on the table. Moments later, another guy in a suit placed two plates in front of us.

I blinked down at the food then up at the guy who moved to stand only a few feet behind Nova, as if he were guarding her or something. It was weird, but she didn't even seem to notice the other guy. Picking up one of the little sandwiches on her plate, she offered it to Ryan, who only gave her a hard look.

She pouted up at him, and he rolled his eyes before taking the sandwich from her and eating it in two bites.

But as adorable as the two of them were, my gaze kept going back to the guy in the suit. The way he was dressed, the stoic, completely emotionless look on his face, even the slight bulge of his jacket that suggested he was carrying a gun, reminded me of the men I'd seen all too often from my bedroom window back at my aunt's house.

Maybe I shouldn't have decided to trust Nova's Ryan so quickly after all.

15

MAX

As soon as we walked through the door of Hannigans', every male eye in the room turned to look at my treasure, and I was ready to go to war with each and every one of the motherfuckers. Ninety percent of them were my MC brothers, but I didn't give a damn. I'd take them all on, put a bullet in each man's head if they even thought about taking Delaney away from me.

I was still gritting my teeth over it when I introduced Delaney to Mom.

The willowy, beautiful blonde who was my mother just stood there, not even blinking as I told her that Delaney was mine. I could see her mind working, taking in how I was standing beside my girl, holding her hand, trying to pull Delaney into me so that I could hide her from the assholes who were already drooling over the gorgeous creature at my side.

I wasn't sure if Mom was stunned by the fact that I cared about a girl enough to want to introduce the two of them, or if she just couldn't understand how such an innocent, amazing little angel could exist in this fucked-up world. But the longer she just stood there, the more tension I could feel coming off Delaney, and it was pissing me off.

Just as I was about to call Mom out on it, she had turned and put her hands up, stopping Aunt Kelli as she demanded I get away from Delaney.

"What the fuck are you doing with her?" she'd yelled, her eyes shooting sparks at me. "Get your blood-covered hands off her!"

"Kelli, cool it," Mom had told her, keeping her voice low and calm. "Just be thankful that we've found her."

What Mom said didn't make sense, but all I could think was that Kelli was trying to take Delaney away from me. I pulled my treasure closer, needing to feel her against me so I didn't lose my fucking mind.

"Let her go!" Kelli yelled. "Give her to me!"

"She's not a fucking doll for me to hand over!" I roared back.

"She's not one of your little playthings either!" she screamed. "We've all seen you with your little whores. I'll be damned if I let you treat my niece like you do them."

Delaney pressed her face into my chest, and I was thankful she couldn't see what the other woman was saying. If Kelli did anything to make my girl think she didn't own me completely, I was going to rip this place apart.

"You think I would introduce any of those idiots to my mom?" I tossed back at her. "Delaney is—" I stopped, my hold on Delaney tightening even more. "Wait. What did you just say?"

Niece?

Delaney was her niece?

"If she's your niece, then why the fuck haven't you been taking care of her?" I bellowed, making half the people in the room flinch as I took a step in Kelli's direction, their gazes ping-ponging between the four of us. Lucky for Kelli, Mom was between us, and I was no longer sure if she was trying to protect Delaney from Kelli, or Kelli from me.

River ran up to her mom, trying to urge her to back away. "Mom, calm down. This isn't getting anyone anywhere. Look. You're scaring Delaney. That's not what we want." The tears in her eyes gave me a moment of pause. I loved my younger cousin, and her tears hurt me just as much as it would if it were Lexa fighting not to cry.

"I couldn't take care of her," Kelli answered me, ignoring River's plea. "Because I didn't even know about her until a few months ago. Her social worker contacted me, but by then, she'd run away from that fucker Tony Garcia. I've been looking for her ever since."

I heard her words, but they made zero impact on my anger. "Not good enough! Your attempts to find her are pathetic because she's been here for weeks. She was out there, lost and alone. Dirty. Cold. *Hungry.*" The word felt like it was torn from my throat, the memory of how I'd found my little treasure like pouring acid on my fucking soul.

"Get out of my way, Raven!" Kelli screeched. "I'm taking my niece home where she belongs."

"She belongs with me!" My voice bounced off the windows, it was so loud, causing the babies in the room to start crying.

Delaney tried to pull away from me, and when I glanced down, it was to find Nova there. Out of the corner of my eye, I saw Ryan, and he gave me a single nod. I knew as long as Nova was in the vicinity, Ryan would be right beside her. If Delaney was with Nova, then she would be safe. Reluctantly, I let her go when she stepped away, wanting her to be away from the crazy bitch trying to steal her from me.

"If you think I'm going to let her stay with you, you've lost your mind," Kelli tossed at me, laughing humorlessly and trying to get around Mom. But as she took a step to the right, Lexa stepped in her way, blocking her path and reinforcing the wall between the two of us. "Out of my way, princess," Kelli seethed.

My sister only crossed her arms, standing nearly half a foot taller than the other woman. Muttering a curse, Kelli moved to go around the other side of Mom, but Tavia was already there, blocking her again. Both my sisters' husbands stood off to the side, holding their children, but watching, ready to step in should either woman need backup.

"Enough." Dad's voice echoed through the room, full of authority that no one could ignore. He stepped between Mom and Kelli, but his blue gaze went straight to me. "I think you should take this outside. Everyone has been given enough of a show tonight. I don't know what's going on, but this is not the time to be airing this shit. That girl—"

"I am that girl's only family besides some skank who was going to put her in one of her husband's whorehouses in Mexico," Kelli gritted out between clenched teeth.

"You only want to protect her. I completely understand. But you were scaring the girl. You mentioned she ran away. Scared people run, Kelli. Calm down before you send her running again." Dad's words seemed to penetrate Kelli's brain because she forced herself to step back.

River pulled her back an extra step. Her movement broke whatever spell everyone else appeared to be under. Maverick moved in, standing at River's back protectively, while Uncle Colt stepped into the chaos.

"Well, at least I know what you and Raven have been up to the last few weeks," he muttered, and she shrugged unashamedly. "I think we should take this discussion outside.

I don't know who Tony is, but he sounds like someone I need to pay a visit to."

"That's why I didn't tell you about it," Kelli snapped at him. "I knew what would happen if you paid that bastard a visit, and it would have put Delaney in even more danger."

Colt opened his mouth, but Dad cut him off. "Take it outside. Raven, you got this?"

She nodded, her hand reaching behind her to grab my shirt, already tugging me toward the door as she kept her eyes trained on Kelli.

I glanced over at where I'd last seen Delaney. Ryan was acting as a shield to her and Nova. A few of his guards were tending to the two girls. Delaney had a drink in one hand, and a plate of food was in front of her that she was snacking on. Knowing she would be safe with them, I followed Mom and Kelli out the door.

We made it five steps into the parking lot before Kelli was in my face. "Where did you find her?"

Mom grabbed her sister-in-law around the waist and forced her back a handful of steps. When there was enough distance between us that she was satisfied, she stepped into Kelli's space. "I understand why you're so upset, and that is the only reason you're not on the ground already. I don't care that you're that girl's only blood family. She's with Max, and that makes her mine now, so don't think for two seconds I won't bury your ass if you keep this shit up."

Kelli blanched and finally realized just who she was dealing with. "Your son is no angel, Raven," she bit out. "I don't want the blood on his hands to touch Delaney."

"There's blood on all of our hands—yours included," Mom shot back. "You aren't going to throw stones at my kid without getting a few slung back at you, Kelli. Now shut your mouth for a minute and let me talk to my boy."

"She was living in the woods," I told Mom as soon as she turned her green eyes on me. "I nearly ran over her on my bike one night on my way home. It was foggy, and she didn't see my light until it was almost too late. I wiped out." Mom's face paled, but I kept going before she could rip into me for not telling her about my wreck. "When I got up, I thought I was dreaming. Or dead. Because all I saw was an angel." I pressed a fist to the center of my chest. "I felt this pressure right here. It doesn't hurt, but when she's not close, I can't breathe."

Her face softened, but she waved her hand, urging me to continue.

"I took her home with me. She'd been on the streets for months, running from her uncle. Tony," I snarled his name and glanced at Kelli. "You don't have to worry about him. I plan on paying the sonofabitch a visit soon."

"How long has she been staying with you?" Kelli demanded, but her voice wasn't nearly as frosty as it had been.

"A little over a week."

"How long have you been fucking her?" she spat the words at my feet, and I had to clench my hands into fists. Hurting a woman went against everything I'd ever been taught, but I wanted to strangle my uncle's wife for the way she was trying to make my relationship with Delaney seem.

"Let's get back on topic," Mom encouraged, trying to defuse my temper. "Tony the pimp was going to put the little deaf angel to work in one of his whorehouses, and baby girl ran away. She is resourceful and old enough to make her own decisions."

My gut began to clench.

"I think we should ask Delaney who she wants to live with."

"No," I growled. "She's mine, and I'm not letting her go."

"She's not a doll, Max." Kelli threw my earlier words back at me. "She's a human being. Let her decide who she would rather put her trust in."

"I agree," Mom said with a sigh. "Delaney needs to know who Kelli is to her."

"I don't care about that. She is more than welcome to explain who she is to Delaney." I raked my hands through my hair, my stomach already protesting because I could see from the gleam in Kelli's eyes that she was going to try to steal my treasure away. "But you aren't taking her from me."

"Max honey, maybe this girl will want to go with Kelli." Mom's voice became consoling. "I mean, she was homeless a week ago. Of course, she wants to be with you right now—"

"No!" I roared. "It's not like that—*she's* not like that. She's with me because she cares about me. I love her, Mom. And I think she loves me too."

"You've known her for a week," Kelli scoffed.

"Don't," I whispered so I didn't yell in her face, then I blinked at my mom when she opened her mouth to no doubt agree with the other woman. "Just don't, Mom. Don't play what I feel for her off as some meaningless infatuation. I've never felt like this before. Lexa fell for Ben fast, too."

"I know that, but Lexa wasn't living on the streets. You've given this girl a roof over her head, food to eat, clothes and jewelry, from the looks of her. That outfit she's wearing didn't come from the Goodwill, Max." She tossed her hands in the air in frustration. "I bet she's even why you bought the Tahoe."

"She is," I confirmed with a nod.

"She went from having nothing to having everything handed to her. If we tell her who Kelli is to her, maybe she will realize that what she's feeling for you is just gratitude."

I straightened my spine. "Fine. Let's tell her. Right now. And I'll show you that you are wrong."

"Max," she said with a sad shake of her head. "I know this is going to be hard."

"No, Mom. You don't know anything, but I'll show you." I turned and lifted my arm toward the bar. "Let's go so you can see what my little treasure is really like."

16

DELANEY

NOVA AND I WEREN'T SITTING THERE LONG BEFORE A SHADOW appeared on the table. Lifting my head, I met the startling blue eyes of Max's sister, Lexa, and his adopted sister, Tavia. Both women and their families were in pictures on the walls of the apartment, so I knew exactly who each one was.

Lexa looked a lot like her brother with her long, glossy black hair, those amazing metallic eyes I loved so much, and the beautiful facial features that belonged on a runway model. Not even the scar on her cheek could distract from how utterly gorgeous she was.

Beside her, Tavia, just as beautiful but looking nothing like her honorary siblings, was assessing me with narrowed eyes.

I gulped, because neither one of them looked particularly welcoming. My heart dropped into my stomach, and I knew they were thinking all the terrible things I'd known they would.

That I wasn't good enough for their brother. That I was just using him.

And even though I'd known down to my bones this was

exactly how his family would react, I'd held out hope they would see that what I felt for Max was real.

Disappointment and hurt had me pushing away the plate of food Ryan's guard had placed in front of me, and I quickly dropped my gaze to the table as shame burned my face.

I felt Nova shifting beside me and chanced lifting my head to find my new friend standing. Her angelic face was scrunched up in displeasure as she confronted the two women in front of her. As tiny as Nova was, they both towered over her, Lexa more so than Tavia, but they each seemed like Amazonians in comparison.

Ryan moved in behind her, his hand going to her shoulder, whether to comfort or to urge her to calm down, I wasn't sure, but his stance was nothing but protective.

Not wanting to watch them—mostly because I didn't want to read the taller women's lips in case they were calling me names, I glanced over to where I'd left Max and his mom now that my view was no longer blocked by Ryan. But Max was no longer there. Neither was his mother or the woman she'd been keeping back.

My gaze went around the room, my heart starting to pound when I couldn't find him anywhere. No, he wouldn't just leave me, I tried to assure myself. He cared about me. He wouldn't abandon me with all these people who so obviously didn't want me there.

But he was gone. I couldn't see him anywhere.

Tears burned my eyes, and I jumped to my feet, needing to be alone. I didn't want anyone to see me break down. They'd already gotten enough of a show on my behalf.

I took two steps, but that was as far as I got before there was a wall of muscle standing in front of me. Blinking in surprise, I looked up into three sets of faces that looked so similar to Max's, my lips fell open in gaped-mouth wonder.

These three had to be related to Max, yet I hadn't seen pictures of any of them on his walls at home.

All three of them were taller than the majority of the other men in the bar, their shoulders just as wide as Max's. The one in the middle seemed to be the oldest, and the one to his left looked more like him than the one on his right, who had three earrings in his left ear and a stud in his nose. At a glance, they were just as beautiful as Max was, but with a second look, I could see they weren't anywhere as close to being as perfect as Max Reid was in my eyes.

It was their eyes that had me completely mesmerized, however. That incredible blue that I could so easily drown in if I weren't careful.

But they didn't belong to the guy I wanted to be wrapped around at that moment. As if they could see the apprehension in my eyes, they stepped closer, blocking me in. But it was the taller of the three, the one standing in the middle, who smiled reassuringly.

To my surprise and complete delight, he lifted his hands and began signing to me. "Hi, I'm Reid." His hands didn't move quite as smoothly as Max's or Nova's did, telling me he wasn't as comfortable or as fluent in ASL as they were, but I was just happy to have someone actually speak to me.

"Delaney," I offered with a small smile.

"Max told me about you," he said, his signs slower, a frown pulling his brows together as he concentrated on the words.

"I can read lips too," I tried to convey, and relief filled his handsome face. "Just talk slowly."

"This is my brother, Elias." He indicated the one on his left, then the one on his right. "And our cousin, Chance." I glanced at the two of them, offering each a tiny smile. Elias gave me a head nod in greeting, but Chance only stood there, his eyes drilling into me, unable to hide his suspiciousness. Just like Tavia and Lexa, only…more intense.

Cautiously, I took a step back from him, and Reid slapped him on the back of the head. "You're scaring her, dumbass," I thought he said, but his lips moved too quickly for me to be sure.

Chance glared at his cousin. "She doesn't belong here. What is Max doing with…"

My tears had dried when these three had appeared in front of me, but they returned at his words. I took another step back, looking away so I didn't have to read the rest of what he was saying. I started to move around him when someone grasped my wrist, turning me to face them.

When my eyes lifted to the bride and her groom, I wanted to sink into the floor. Her eyes were glassy with tears, and the tip of her nose was red. She had reason to cry and even to be angry with me. Having me show up with Max had ruined her wedding reception. She was probably going to make me leave, and I was all too ready to go.

Yet when I expected her to drag me toward the door, she jerked me against her with surprising strength and wrapped her arms around me in a hug so tight, it knocked the air from my lungs.

Shocked, I stood there, my arms at my sides, not sure what to do next.

The hug lasted all of twenty seconds before she released me, and then she was smiling at me as tears spilled down her cheeks. Her mouth moved so fast I couldn't make out a single word. Unable to follow her, I glanced at the tall, kind of scary guy behind her.

Recognition hit me, and I realized he worked at the Ink Shoppe. I'd only seen glimpses of him in the weeks before

I'd met Max, but it was hard not to recognize a guy who looked like him.

Which meant…

I threw my arms around the bride, tears spilling down my cheeks just as rapidly as they were hers. My hug didn't last nearly as long as hers had, but when I pulled back, I was quick to sign what was in my heart.

My appreciation and gratitude for what she'd been able to do for me when she hadn't had to do anything but call the cops on me for squatting in her place of work at night.

When she just stood there, frowning at me because she was unable to keep up with what I was saying, I swallowed the lump in my throat and spoke the words. "Thank you. For…for the…blanket."

Her green eyes widened even more, understanding lighting her entire face, and then we were hugging again.

"It was you?" I read her lips when she pulled her head back. "You…?"

Shame hit me again, but I nodded. "I'm sorry if…I got you into…trouble."

"You didn't," she said with a shake of her head. "I have been so worried about you. But you've been with Max?"

"For a little while."

"Oh." Turning her head, she looked up at the guy behind her. He gave her a grim smile, and she seemed to relax a little. The connection I could sense between them reminded me of how it was between Max and me.

I glanced around, hoping to see him, but when he didn't magically appear, my heart sank all over again.

"I should go," I spoke again. The vibrations in my throat from speaking so much were weird, and I hoped she could understand me. When her head snapped around to look at me again, I saw something like determination swimming in her eyes. "I'm sorry…for ruining today for you."

"No, no. You didn't. I swear. This has been a great wedding present. Finding you." She clutched at both of my hands, holding them tightly in her grip. "Mom has been looking everywhere for you, Delaney."

Maybe I was reading her lips wrong, because no way was her mom looking for me. If her mother was the woman Raven had to hold back earlier as I suspected, then I was sure of it. Why would she even care about me, the homeless girl who had been bothering everyone in town?

Unless…

Did she work for Uncle Tony and Aunt June?

It seemed impossible, but my uncle was a bad man. It was reasonable to believe he had contacts everywhere.

I jerked out of the bride's hold—River, I remembered Max saying his cousin's name was—and started backing away from her.

"What's wrong?" River demanded, her face scrunching up and reminding me a little of Nova. "Don't be afraid. I'm sorry. I didn't—"

Her mouth stopped moving, and she glanced at something over my shoulder. Before I could turn to see what the new danger was, strong arms wrapped around me from behind. My eyes clenched closed as relief hit me so hard, I could actually taste it.

Max.

He hadn't left me.

I didn't know where he'd gone, but he hadn't abandoned me.

My knees felt weak as I turned in his arms and buried my face in his chest, inhaling his comforting scent and letting the safety of his hold calm my racing heart. His hands rubbed up and down my back, erasing the hurt I'd felt when I first thought he'd left me there to deal with his family all on my own.

His thumb under my chin tipped my head up moments later, making me look up at him. "Okay?" he mouthed the words.

I shrugged, not sure if I was or not. My fear that his family would hate me had come true, and now River was telling me her mom had been looking for me. I was scared and confused, my heart still aching knowing people thought I was only using him.

He stroked one hand over my hair, tucking a few strands behind my ear and exposing the earrings that matched the necklace he'd insisted I wear. They were light as air, but right then, they felt like they weighed my head down, making it impossible to lift it high under the weight of the money he'd spent on me, while everyone who looked at me judged me.

Max pressed his lips to my forehead before releasing me so he could sign, "Come outside with me. We need to talk."

In every book I'd ever read, I knew that those four words never led to anything good. Apprehensively, I let him take my hand and followed him out the door, mostly because I just wanted to be away from all the angry looks everyone was shooting me.

But when we stepped outside and I saw his mom standing close by with the angry woman from earlier, I stopped in my tracks. I didn't feel up to whatever was going to happen, and I knew before either of them even took a step toward us that something was about to.

"It's okay," he tried to reassure me, urging me forward. "I'm right here."

He'd said that earlier too, but he hadn't been anywhere when his sisters had tried to confront me and then his cousin

Chance had let me know I didn't belong. Where was he when I needed him?

From the looks of it, he'd been outside with these two women.

Had they told him to send me packing?

Was that what we needed to *talk* about?

Was he about to let me down gently while his mom watched?

Max kept walking forward, taking me with him. I wanted to drag my feet, but what was the use? If he wanted to get rid of me, then I just wanted to get it over and done with.

He stopped several feet from where the others were standing before turning and signing, "I have something to tell you. It came as a huge surprise to me too, and that was why everything got crazy inside." He paused and inhaled deeply before blowing it out in a rush. "This is my aunt Kelli. She's married to my uncle Colt, Mom's brother."

I glanced over at the brunette, and she gave a small, almost shy wave. Her face was pale, her eyes glittering with a mixture of emotions I didn't understand, but she didn't seem angry like she had earlier. Tentatively, I waved back.

"Okay, first things first," Max continued once my gaze was back on him. "Did you know that your mom was adopted?"

I frowned at the weird subject change. "Yes. It wasn't something she kept from me. Her parents were unable to have children of their own, so they adopted her. But they died when I was a baby." I didn't even remember my grandparents, but from the pictures I'd seen of them before the passing of my own parents, it was easy to tell that they had loved my mom.

"When you went to live with your aunt and uncle, your social worker was concerned for you. She spent the last eight years researching your mom's family in hopes of finding someone else she could possibly place you with so you wouldn't have to live with Garcia." Max pointed to Kelli. "And she found Kelli. Your mom's biological father was also hers."

The news struck me dead center, like getting hit with a wrecking ball, knocking the oxygen from my lungs. I stumbled back a few steps, but Max was there to catch and steady me.

"What…?" I signed, then stopped, unsure what to even say.

"She's your mom's sister. Half sister," he amended. "But still your aunt. The social worker contacted her, but by that time, you had already run away."

"Mom has been looking everywhere for you, Delaney."

River's words from only minutes before replayed in my head, and understanding finally clicked in my brain. Her mom wasn't looking for me because she worked for Uncle Tony, but because she was my aunt.

The fear that I'd felt began to ease a little, and I glanced at Kelli again. As if taking that as permission, she stepped up beside Max, but he took a step closer to me, putting more distance between me and…my aunt.

I had another aunt besides Aunt June.

That realization was kind of bizarre to me. It was weird to find another family member.

But then again, it had been just as much so when I'd met Aunt June the first time after the death of my parents.

"You…didn't know my mom at all?" I signed.

Not understanding what I'd just said, Kelli looked up at Max to translate.

"She wants to know if you knew her mom," he said while signing the words so I knew what was being said.

"No," I could read her answer, but Max still translated for her. "I didn't even know she existed until a few months ago when the social worker called to tell me about you."

"Oh." I didn't know why I was disappointed. With her having only just found out about me, there was little chance she would have known my mom, but it would have been nice to have someone to talk about her with. Someone who had memories from her childhood and could tell me about the woman I missed with my whole heart.

"I wish I had known her," Kelli spoke after a small pause. "I grew up as an only child. I had a half brother, but he was…" Her mouth twisted in distaste. "Let's just say he wasn't worth knowing. But I would have liked to have had a sister growing up. Maybe…you could tell me about her?"

I immediately started nodding, my heart lifting with happiness. I wouldn't get to know someone else's memories of Mom, but I would get to share my own. And they were great memories. I'd had to live off them for the past eight years, and they had kept me going when I was at my loneliest.

"Delaney," Max signed my name, pulling my gaze to him. Having him call me that and not "treasure" made me flinch. He knew what I wanted him to call me, so why was he using my given name instead? Was he embarrassed to call me his treasure when he was in front of other people—in front of his mom?

"Kelli wants you to come live with her."

As he formed each word with his hands, his face remained emotionless, and I suddenly felt cold. Wrapping my arms around myself, I stood there looking up at him, waiting for him to tell me what *he* wanted.

The Max I knew and loved wasn't standing in front of me. This guy was a stranger to me, with his cold, blank eyes and impassive facial expression. I couldn't read him, and that hurt more than when I thought he'd abandoned me earlier.

My Max seemed to have disappeared, making me wonder if he was real or just a figment of my imagination. Maybe I'd misunderstood what was between us.

He didn't speak, didn't even move a finger to sign a single word. That was when I knew what he wanted and what I had to do.

"No," I told him, and he seemed to jerk in reaction.

His nostrils flared, the first sign of any emotion from him since he'd said my name. He reached for me, but I backed away, focusing on Kelli. "I'm sorry. I can't." I signed the words, unable to speak for the lump that was choking me. "I want to get to know you, but I think it would be better if we do that slowly. I don't think I'm ready to trust anyone else right now."

Kelli looked at me in confusion, and I realized Max hadn't translated for me. Looking up at him, I found him frowning at me, his metallic-blue eyes glittering with an emotion I wasn't ready to decipher. All I knew was that I didn't want to see disappointment in his gaze.

He didn't have to worry. Just because I'd turned down Kelli's offer to move in with her didn't mean he would have to continue to deal with me.

I understood. He wanted me to go with Kelli. I knew his mom was probably the one who'd made him realize I was no good for him. Not that I could blame her. Max deserved so much better than me.

It was okay, though.

I would be okay.

And I would make this easy for him.

17

MAX

"No."

The relief I felt at that one word nearly brought me to my knees. I knew Delaney wouldn't let me down, but I'd felt a sliver of doubt that had made me hold my breath while I waited for her reaction to finding out Kelli was able and willing to give her all the things she needed.

But when I reached for my treasure, she stepped back, the hurt shining like twin spotlights from her brown eyes.

"I'm sorry, I can't." She signed as she glanced over at Kelli. "I want to get to know you, but I think it would be better if we do that slowly. I don't think I'm ready to trust anyone else right now."

"What did she say?" Kelli hissed beside me, her confusion thick in her voice, but I couldn't look away from my treasure.

I was afraid if I so much as blinked, she would disappear.

"She said she wants to take things slow because she's not ready to trust anyone else right now," Mom translated for her. "Which is completely understandable. I'm sure her aunt and uncle gave her some serious trust issues."

"I guess you're right," Kelli mumbled. "Hell, I need to just be thankful that we found her and she's safe. I was totally turning into Colt there for a minute. I'm sorry."

"It's fine," Mom told her. "At least you didn't pull some shitty stunt like my idiot brother did the other night."

"Fuck. If I get that bad, knock some sense into me," Kelli laughed.

"Trust me, I will."

Snickering, Kelli walked over to Delaney. "Can I…hug you?" she asked slowly.

After only a small hesitation, Delaney nodded. Kelli pulled her niece into a tight hug, making my girl squeak at how hard she was being squeezed. "Sorry, sorry," Kelli said as she lifted her head from Delaney's shoulder. "Did I hurt you?"

She shook her head, offering a tiny smile that didn't reach her eyes.

"Thank you for giving me a chance to get to know you," Kelli said, keeping her words slow so Delaney could under-stand her. "When my mom died, I lost the last of my family. Finding you… Well, I don't feel as alone in the world anymore."

My treasure's face softened. "I understand," she signed, and I translated for her. "I felt like I lost part of myself when my parents died."

"Exactly," Kelli agreed, hugging her again.

It was Delaney who pulled back first. "You should get back inside. I'm keeping you from your daughter's wedding reception."

Kelli signed heavily. "This is a pretty huge deal for her. And I've already caused a scene that the entire town will be talking about for weeks." She cupped one side of Delaney's face. "But I want you to know, no matter what, I'm here if you need me." She shot me a glare over her shoulder, but I ignored it and continued to translate for her as she spoke. "No matter what happens between you and Max."

"Thank you," Delaney spoke the words aloud, her voice barely above a whisper.

With one more hug, Kelli went back into the bar, leaving me alone with just my mom and my treasure.

As the door closed behind my aunt, Delaney lifted her hands and began taking off her earrings. Watching her gave me a jolt. I wanted to tell her to put them back on, but I suddenly couldn't remember how to work my tongue. Crossing the space that separated us, she took my hand and dropped them into my palm before reaching behind her to unclasp her necklace.

I stood there, frozen, as I watched the glittery stones sparkle in the late-afternoon sunlight.

"Yesterday when Max took me to the mall, I saw a sign for a women's shelter at the edge of town," she signed to Mom. "I hadn't been to that area before, so I didn't know there was a shelter here."

Mom and I glanced at each other, her gaze full of surprise, mine of trepidation. Fuck, I knew in my gut what was coming.

"You don't have to worry. I won't bother your son anymore," Delaney continued when we both turned our eyes back on her. "I can see now this was all a really big mistake."

"No!" I exploded, reaching for her. She couldn't leave me.

But she was expecting it and jumped back from my touch. "I knew you and your family would disapprove of me." She spoke directly to Mom, refusing to even look at me. "I mean, who wants their son to be with some homeless girl, right?" She gave a brittle smile, trying to make light of the situation.

But the smile only lasted a second before her chin began to tremble.

Blinking back tears, she walked around Mom, moving toward the road.

"Give her the choice," I growled, glaring at Mom as I stuffed Delaney's jewelry in my pants pocket. "Let her know she has options, you said."

"I just wanted her to know—"

"You wanted to test her!" I roared.

She put her hands on her hips. "Yes," she admitted unabashedly. "The good news is, she passed. The bad news, it backfired. Now, stop snarling at me and go get her!"

But I was already running after my treasure.

She hadn't even reached the end of the parking lot before I scooped her up and tossed her over my shoulder. With a squeak, she struggled against me. Ignoring her attempts to get free, I stomped past my mom to the Tahoe and dropped her into the passenger seat. Keeping her in place with one hand on her chest, I fastened the seat belt around her.

"You aren't going anywhere," I informed her, my jaw clenched so hard, I thought it might lock. "Except home where you belong."

When she started to argue, I captured her mouth in a hard kiss. My fear of losing her, of her walking away from me and never getting to hold her again, made me rough, and I had to force myself to release her. Lifting my head, I stepped back and slammed the door closed.

"Call me later!" Mom yelled as she watched us.

I didn't answer as I got into the driver's seat and started the engine. Wasting no time, I drove us home, trying to figure out what I was going to say to her to make her understand she belonged with me.

During the drive, Delaney remained motionless, her gaze

focused directly out the windshield, her hands folded in her lap. I shot her glances every few seconds, desperate to know what she was thinking, but she didn't spare me a single look in return. Not even a damn side-eye.

Parking the Tahoe, I got out and jogged around to open her door, but she was already out before I reached the passenger door. Breathing hard, I gently took her hand, and we walked upstairs to the apartment.

After unlocking the door, I nudged her in ahead of me.

Delaney didn't hesitate to go inside, but instead of pausing in the living room, she walked into the bedroom. Pulling off her new dress, she went to the closet and changed into a pair of cheap jeans and a tank top.

The sight of her in nothing but her bra and panties had my tongue glued to the roof of my mouth as all the blood in my body surged into my dick. But then she folded the dress, placing it on the floor beside the ballet flats she'd kicked off before grabbing the old backpack she'd had with her when I found her that first night.

Without sparing me another glance, she turned and walked back the way she'd come less than five minutes before.

Realizing she was leaving me, I ran after her.

By the time I caught up with her, she was nearly to the front door. My breaths were coming in hard pants, my hands shaking, my skin feeling like it was too tightly stretched across my muscles. Fearing that if I didn't get between her and the door, I would lose her forever, I grasped Delaney's hips and twisted us.

My back hit the door, blocking her exit, but my panic didn't ease.

"Don't go," I pleaded.

But she wasn't even looking at me. Her head was turned

to the side, her eyes focused on the wall, blocking me out completely.

When I continued to cut off her exit, she finally lifted her eyes to look at me. "Please move. I don't belong here."

My heart felt like she was physically ripping it out of my chest. "Treasure—"

"I'm "treasure' now?" she demanded, the hurt shining out of her eyes like a punch to the gut. "Funny how you forgot that when we were in front of your family."

"No," I denied. "You are my treasure. Now and always."

"As long as your mom or sisters aren't around," she signed with a nod.

"No!"

"Admit it," she commanded. "You and I do not belong together. Your family made that obvious tonight, and I finally opened my eyes to that fact." She paused, then shook her head. "No, that's a lie. I always knew this wouldn't work. You're you, and I'm…me. Your mom, your sisters and cousins, they took one look at me, and they knew what I've been denying from the night we met. I was only deluding myself, imagining that we stood a chance just because I fell in love with you."

My heart stopped, the air seeming to freeze in my lungs. "You love me?" I wheezed out, and thank fuck her eyes were on my mouth because my brain didn't have enough firepower to speak to her in ASL right then.

Her eyes filled with tears, but she squared her shoulders. "Yes," she signed, lifting her chin and meeting my gaze. "But it doesn't matter. Love isn't enough when there are such drastic differences between us."

She was right. There were huge differences between the two of us. She was an angel, so innocent and beautiful inside and out. Whereas I could kill a man and not feel an ounce of remorse. I was evil compared to her kind soul.

My treasure thought she was wrong for me because she had lived on the streets. She assumed that because she had no money or material things that she wasn't good enough for me. She was willing to let me go because she thought my family disapproved of us being together.

And the worst part was, even though I knew that I should let her go, that I was wrong for her in all the worst ways, I couldn't. I was too selfish. I needed Delaney more than I needed anything or anyone.

I would die before I willingly gave her up.

"What did my sisters do?" I asked, needing to know so I could fix whatever they must have unintentionally done to make her think we were wrong for each other. I frowned, because she'd mentioned my cousins as well. "Which cousins made you think we shouldn't be together."

"It doesn't matter," she dismissed. "Get out of my way, Max. I never should have even come here with you that first night. You should have just taken me to that shelter."

"That shelter is for battered women on the run from their abusive boyfriends or husbands," I told her. Of course, it was for runaways too, but she didn't need to know that anytime soon. "My aunt Gracie runs it."

She blanched, taking a step back from me. "Your family runs this entire town, don't they? The diner, this garage, the sheriff, that bar, even the shelter." Swallowing hard, she adjusted the strap of the backpack on her shoulder. "What else do they control?"

"It's not a big deal."

"It is to me."

"It's not so much my biological family that controls the county." Her eyes narrowed on me, and I sighed, knowing the truth wasn't going to win me any points. My family did basically own Trinity County in some shape or form, but not exactly all of it. The college wasn't owned, operated, or even on our agenda. If anything, it was a pain in the ass, but one that brought economic growth to the community when school was in session. "Most of the small businesses in town are owned and operated by at least one member of my MC."

"Of course they are," she signed, her head shaking disparagingly. "You're not only the sweetest, kindest guy I've ever met, but you're also like the prince of this place. You're royalty, and I'm… I'm…" A tear spilled over her lashes. "I'm just the trash that needs to be taken out."

Her words broke my heart and pissed me off all at the same time. Picking her up, I made sure the door was locked before carrying her back into our bedroom. Shutting and locking that door as well, I crossed to the bed and placed her on the end before dropping to my knees in front of her.

"Pay attention," I instructed. "Because I need you to really understand what I'm saying here."

Her chin trembled, but she nodded.

"Do not ever refer to yourself as trash. Not now, not ever." Her teeth sank into her bottom lip, and I used my thumb to release the tortured flesh. I wanted to kiss the teeth imprints away, but I needed to get this sorted with her before I put my lips on her again. "I am unworthy of you and your beautiful soul, treasure. The moment I set eyes on you, I knew that angels were real because one had fallen from heaven and stood before me. I thought I'd died, but when I realized I would have been dragged to hell, not given a taste of paradise in the form of you, I knew I was still very much alive."

Her brows pinched together. "You couldn't possibly be sent to hell," she tried to argue.

I wanted to laugh, but she didn't know the darker side of my life. If she did, she would never think I was sweet or kind. But she wouldn't have been so misled into thinking that I was better than her either. In comparison, I was worthless. Anyone who knew the real me would see that in two seconds flat.

Guilt should have weighed me down for not showing her who I really was, but I was a selfish bastard. I wanted her blinders to remain on. I hoped she only ever saw the good in me, that small flicker of light that still lived inside me. I could fan the flames of that part of myself for her, make it bigger and bigger until one day I might be worthy of her. Until then, I would hide my darkness from her.

If I had to hide the darkness for the rest of my life, so be it.

"What did my cousins say?" I asked, pulling her focus on to a more important topic. She shrugged and looked away, trying to avoid the conversation, but I wasn't about to allow that shit. Tipping her chin back to look at me, I asked her again. "Which cousin, and what did he say?"

She released a tiny huff, making me smile. "The one with the nose ring," she signed. "Chance?"

Gritting my teeth, I nodded, knowing exactly who she was talking about. Of course it was Chance, the fucker.

18

MAX

"HE TOLD REID THAT I HAD NO BUSINESS WITH YOU, OR something like that. I stopped looking after that."

I threw my head back, laughing so hard my sides hurt. This girl, she was so ready to believe people thought she was the reason we didn't belong together. If she'd kept reading Chance's lips, I knew she would have discovered a hell of a lot about that particular cousin's opinion of me.

She slapped her hand against my chest, her eyes glittering with hurt and effectively stopping my laughter. "It isn't funny!"

"Ah, baby, if you only knew, you would be hysterical with laughter, trust me." Leaning forward, I touched my lips to her forehead before pulling back enough to sign. "I completely believe that Chance said that. But I doubt it was in the same context as you think it was."

Her brow scrunched up. "How could it mean anything but *exactly* that? He doesn't think we should be together. None of your family does."

"Believe me when I say that Chance wasn't worried about me when he said what he did. He hates me, and the feeling is mutual for the most part," I told her truthfully. "We've never gotten along. There hasn't been a single time we've been in the same room and not argued or even gone at each other's throats. Our moms say it's because we're too much alike." I shrugged. "Don't tell them this, but I think they're right. There isn't really a reason for us not to get along. We grew up in houses side by side. I love him, but I hate him. If I'm in a jam, there really aren't many other people I would want to have my back. But I swear to you, on my mother's life—and I don't take that shit lightly, treasure—Chance was most likely looking out for you and not me."

Her expression turned skeptical. "You're trying to tell me that he thinks we have no business being together because you're not good enough for me?" I nodded emphatically, but she pushed at my shoulders angrily. "No. I don't believe that for a second. That is ridiculous. I don't care how much you two dislike each other, there is no way that guy was worried for me."

Frustrated that she didn't believe me, I scrubbed my hands over my face. "What do you need me to do to prove it to you, babe?" I asked when I looked at her again. "Do you want me to find the little asshole and make him confirm what I'm saying is the truth?"

Her plump lips pressed into a hard line, her eyes narrowing on me angrily.

"I will if that's what you need." Fuck, I'd beat the shit out of him and then throw him at her feet—before I made him tell her that was exactly what he meant when he was running his mouth.

"Fine," she signed, rolling her eyes. "Maybe that was what your cousin meant. But what about your sisters? They obviously didn't think I was good enough. They tried to confront me, but Nova stopped them."

"What did they say?" I couldn't help growling the words as I signed them for her. I loved my sisters, but if whatever they'd said or done caused me to lose my treasure, I would never forgive either of them.

"I don't know!" She glanced down at her hands for a moment before continuing. "I wasn't brave enough to stick around to find out what they thought of me. But with the way Nova was reacting to whatever Lexa and Tavia were saying, she wasn't happy."

Cursing, I pulled my phone out of my pants pocket. I could have called either of my sisters, but I knew if I spoke to either of them and they admitted to doing something to hurt my girl, I would end up saying something I couldn't take back. Hitting connect on Nova's name, I waited.

Two rings later and I heard her voice. "Is Delaney okay?"

"What did Lexa and Tavia say or do to make her think either of them doesn't like her?" I demanded.

There was a short pause on her end before she snickered. "Okay, I'm sorry. That's insane. Neither one of them even came close to doing something like that." I heard a deep voice in the background, and Nova's voice became slightly muffled as she spoke to Ryan. "Well, I mean... Yeah, okay, you're right."

"What?" I barked.

"It's just that the way Lexa and Tavia came up on us, I guess it could have scared Delaney. They had that fierce look on their faces, and now that I think about it, I realize those two can be beyond intimidating if you don't know them." She sighed. "Which Delaney doesn't."

"Just tell me everything that happened, Nova."

"We were sitting there eating, and those two came up to us. I jumped up and told them both not to overwhelm Delaney," she explained. "They were so excited that you found a girl you care about enough to bring to a family event, and they were really animated. I swear, they didn't say anything that would make her think they didn't like her. If anything, it would have been the opposite. But of course, she couldn't hear any of that. Ryan said while I was trying to contain Lexa and Tavia, that Reid, Elias, and Chance spoke to her. Chance, of course, started running his mouth while Reid was talking to her, and Reid started slapping Chance around." She made a pained sound. "Ugh, I'm sorry. I should have taken better care of her."

"No," I cut in. "I should have been there to take care of her myself. Maybe then she wouldn't be trying to fucking leave me right now."

"Do you want me to come speak to her?" Nova offered.

I looked up at Delaney, who was watching me intently, her eyes glued to my mouth. "No," I turned my head and spoke into the phone, keeping Delaney from seeing my lips as they moved. "I'll get this straightened out. But make Aunt Gracie understand that if Delaney shows up at the shelter, she needs to tell her they don't have any beds available."

Nova gasped. "Max! No. I won't do it. If Delaney leaves, then she needs somewhere she will feel safe. Right now, it's obvious she doesn't trust any of us. I won't be a part of taking that option away from her."

"Fine," I muttered, fighting back a round of curses. "I'll call Jack and tell him."

"Stop it, Max," Nova hissed. "Do you want her to trust you or not? Because if I were her, I definitely wouldn't at the moment. This is not how you keep people you care about. You're supposed to be open and honest. And if they don't want to be around you because they're hurt or angry, you let them have a moment—or a freaking week—to themselves if that's what they need."

She was right, but that didn't mean I wouldn't make it harder for my treasure to leave me. I wasn't known for playing fair, and I sure as fuck wouldn't change now when I was fighting to keep the one person I knew I couldn't live without.

"Have fun in New York, Nova," I told her. "See you at the end of the summer."

"Asshole," I heard her grumble before I ended the call.

Instead of calling my cousin Jack, I texted him. Before I even had time to look back at Delaney, I got a confirmation from him that he would take care of it should the situation arise.

Pocketing my phone, I turned my gaze on my girl, only to find her beautiful face had completely shut down. I couldn't read anything she was feeling in her eyes, her normally expressive face closed off. I knew she couldn't have heard what I'd just told Nova, and my mouth had been covered so she couldn't read my lips. I'd kept the screen of my phone out of her line of vision, so I knew she didn't read the text I'd sent to my cousin or his reply.

"Baby, what's wrong?"

She pushed me back and got to her feet. "I think I'll take my chances at the shelter after all."

"Fuck!" I bellowed, and I was thankful she couldn't hear me because I probably would have scared her.

I caught her around the waist with one arm before she even got to the door. The noises that left my throat sounded like those of a wounded animal, and I wasn't completely sure that I wasn't. Just the thought of her leaving was enough to make my entire body shake as agony spread through my veins like poison.

Dropping her on the bed, I followed her down, already ripping her T-shirt down the middle. She couldn't leave if she didn't have anything to wear. I would start with the clothes she had on, and once I'd fucked her into a coma, I would destroy everything else so she wouldn't be able to so much as step outside.

Delaney's mouth fell open in shock as I tossed her ruined shirt over my shoulder. Grabbing her bra, I tore it apart, sending the shredded material flying as well. Her breathing picked up, coming in heavy pants. But I didn't see fear in her eyes. They were ablaze with need, her nipples diamond hard as her tits strained toward me, practically begging for my attention.

I was rough as I undid her jeans and peeled them off her body. I'd deal with them as soon as she was asleep. Maybe I would put all her clothes in a pile and burn them. Whatever the fuck I had to do in order to keep my treasure, I wouldn't hesitate to accomplish.

But first, I needed to feel her clenching around my cock as she came over and over again for me.

Dipping my fingers into each side of her already soaked panties, I twisted the digits and heard the satisfying tear as they practically disintegrated with just a little exertion.

Not daring to waste time, I tore open my pants and pushed them and my boxer briefs down my hips just enough to free my aching cock. Reaching into the bedside drawer, I grabbed a condom and sheathed myself before thrusting into her tight pussy.

"Yes!" Delaney cried out, her body bowing in pleasure as she scraped her nails down my back so hard, I felt blood dripping in their wake. I knew my grin must have been predatory, but she was too lost in the sensations only I'd ever given her.

"Max," she moaned my name, clinging to me like I was her lifeline. "So…close."

Her walls were already clenching my cock like a tight fist,

her entire body convulsing from the force of her first orgasm, but I didn't let up. I wanted her so sedated she couldn't keep her eyes open.

My own release tried to sneak up on me, but I bit down on my wrist, fighting it so I could fuck my girl into oblivion.

She came three more times before her eyes began to drift closed, and she struggled to keep them open. "Thank fuck," I groaned, pistoning my hips as I finally let go and found relief.

Out of breath, I fell onto my side, taking her with me. Locking my arms and legs around her small body, I held her close for a long while. I wasn't sure how much time passed before I untangled myself from around her and tucked the covers up to her chin. She made a little mewling sound as she buried her head deeper into the pillow.

Dropping a kiss on her brow, I stood, pulled off the full condom, and fixed my clothes. After disposing of the used contraceptive, I grabbed all of her clothes and shoved them into a garbage bag. Finding the lighter in the kitchen, I opened the front door, ready to burn Delaney's clothes in the parking lot, only to come face-to-face with Lexa and Tavia.

My biological sister looked down at what was in my hands, her dark brows lifting toward the sky. "What are you doing, little brother?"

I shrugged. "Going to have a bonfire in the parking lot."

"That's her shit, huh?" I didn't answer, and she smirked. "I guess if you want to keep someone inside, that's better than handcuffs. Unless they don't care to walk around naked."

Tavia huffed disapprovingly. "You're already fucking it up, dumbass. You don't keep a girl by forcing her to stay." She grabbed the bag out of my hand while Lexa pushed me back inside the apartment. Once they were both across the threshold, Tavia slammed the door shut. "We're here to make sure you don't lose Delaney. Now, sit down and listen."

I just stood there, glaring at them both. "It's because of you two that she thinks we shouldn't be together. You made her think you don't approve of her and that she's not good enough."

They shared a quick look.

"We didn't mean to," Lexa assured me as she moved farther into the living room. "We were just so happy to see you with someone who isn't some slutty sorority bitch. I admit we came on a little strong when we tried to talk to her, but Nova set us straight, and we backed off to give her time to breathe."

"Well, now she thinks you don't like her, and she's convinced herself that she's not good enough for me." I tried to grab the garbage bag from Tavia, but she was a quick little thing and jumped behind Lexa. "Damn it, Tav. I'm just trying to keep her from leaving me."

"Back up." Lexa waved her hands in a rewind kind of motion. "Did you just say that sweet girl thinks *she* isn't good enough for *you*?"

"You heard me just fine," I snapped at her, my frustration bleeding through.

She burst out laughing. "Hell, we came just in time, Tavia."

"I know," the younger woman agreed, shaking her head in mock despair. "I'm glad we told the husbands to hold back and let us talk to him first."

"Fuck," I muttered to myself, not looking forward to either of my brothers-in-law knocking on my door. Knowing I had little choice but to hear what my sisters had to say unless I wanted to physically put them outside— which would only lead to bloodshed that I wasn't confident wouldn't be my own staining my carpets—I dropped onto the couch. "Okay, get on with it. Spit out what you want to say and then send in the sheriff and the Russian crime lord."

"*Hmph*," Tavia said with a shake of her head. "You make it sound like our husbands are the scary ones. When it's us you need to worry about kicking your ass."

"Definitely!" Lexa agreed as the two of them moved so they were standing side by side and glaring down at me. "And we don't even have anything to say to you, anyway. Nova told us all about your plan to have Jack turn poor Delaney away if she showed up. You're lucky we didn't rat you out to Mom or Aunt Gracie. Otherwise, they would have shown up here and already kicked your balls into your throat."

"You came to talk to Delaney?" They both nodded, and I relaxed. "Good. You two can talk her out of leaving. But if you hurt her feelings again, or say anything that makes her want to leave me even more than she already does, I'll never speak to either of you again."

"Damn, that sounds like a great reason to do just that," Lexa muttered to Tavia. "Too bad I already like this Delaney girl."

Tavia elbowed her in the side. "Don't even joke about this. I know what it's like to feel all alone in the world. I refuse to do anything to make her feel even worse just to score points off this idiot."

Remorse filled my older sister's eyes. "You're right. I'm sorry." Leaning down, she grabbed my arm and tugged. "Ben and Theo are waiting outside. They need to speak to you."

"Great," I grumbled. "Are they going to kick my ass?"

"As much fun as that would be to watch, no," Tavia informed me. "Gian recognized a name that got thrown out when all hell was breaking loose between you and Kelli earlier. Don't ask me who or what it is about. Theo doesn't tell me anything when it comes to 'business.'" She rolled her eyes as she made air quotes at the last word. "But it seemed important, so you need to go deal with them before they drag your ass out there for this little powwow."

The only name I could remember being mentioned earlier was when Kelli had brought up Tony Garcia. Anger hit me hard just thinking the bastard's name, but I turned at the door, staring my sisters down. "I mean it. You two better not make so much as a single tear fall from her pretty eyes. And if my treasure isn't here when I get back—"

"Aww!" they gushed at the same time. "That's the most adorable pet name I've ever heard," Lexa fawned. "I had no idea my baby brother was such a romantic."

"I mean it!" I yelled, forcing them to snap out of their girlie moment. "No tears, and she better be here when I get back. Understand?"

"We heard you, Max." Lexa pushed me out the door. "Now go, so we can work a little magic on your treasure."

19

———

DELANEY

I JERKED AWAKE, MY HEART POUNDING AGAINST MY RIBS, AND reached for Max, needing his arms around me as a wave of fear left me trembling. I barely remembered the dream I'd just had, and it was quickly fading from my mind as my hands patted the bed in the dark and only came into contact with Max's pillow.

All I could remember was the urgency to run, like the night Marta had come into my room, telling me I needed to go. Even though it had been there this entire time, the sense of danger hadn't been nearly as strong between that night and now. I wasn't sure why it was suddenly pushing down on me, but the need to get as far away as fast as possible was beginning to make my stomach churn.

Trying to calm my racing heart, I pulled Max's pillow to my chest and buried my face in it, inhaling his scent in a desperate attempt to calm myself. It was just a dream, I tried to reassure myself. After the events of the day, it was hitting me harder than it normally would.

That was what I kept telling myself, but I wasn't sure I

154

believed it. There was just a niggling feeling in the back of my mind that kept whispering for me to run.

After a few minutes, I sat up and tossed the pillow aside. It was dark outside the window, and my stomach was growling with hunger. I couldn't smell food, but Max always had us something to eat by now. Given how long we'd made love earlier, I knew he must have been hungry. And with how much of a workout he put us both through each time, it was no wonder he was always so ravenous.

Flipping on a light, I crossed to the closet to get dressed. Max had shredded my clothes in his haste to get me naked, and it had turned my blood to lava watching his desperate rush to get my body bared for his hands and lips. It was the first time he'd shown me that side of himself, and I wanted more of it. It was hot, and the possessiveness that had shone from his eyes had told me how much he wanted me more than anything else ever had.

When I opened the closet door, the smile that had begun to lift my lips at the memory dropped at the sight before me. The hangers where my clothes had been were now bare. All that was left were Max's things. My gaze lowered to the floor, thinking maybe I'd knocked everything over earlier when I'd changed out of my dress and grabbed my backpack. But no, the floor only had a few pairs of shoes. And other than the flats I'd worn to the reception, the rest were Max's.

My heart, which had been so full only moments before, cracked open. Had Max changed his mind? Did he not want me to stay after all? Had our lovemaking been his way of telling me we really were over?

When I'd fallen asleep in his arms after he'd blown my mind countless times, I'd decided I wouldn't care what his family thought as long as he wanted me around. But by the looks of it, he'd already packed me up. No doubt he was waiting for me to wake up so he could take me to the women's shelter.

But he hadn't even left me a single thing to change into. That was so unlike Max that it gave me a moment of pause. If he wanted to get me out of his life, he would have at least left an outfit for me to wear.

Confused, I grabbed one of his shirts and pulled it on, then found a pair of his boxers. Finger-combing my hair, I left the bedroom. In the living room, I came to a sudden halt when I saw the two beautiful women sitting on the couch.

Their heads snapped up, and their faces brightened, which only confused me. Lexa was the first to get to her feet. "We didn't get a chance to introduce ourselves earlier," she began, signing effortlessly. "I'm Lexa, and this is Tavia."

Unsure what to say, I shyly waved to them both.

"I want to apologize for earlier," Lexa continued. "We were so happy to see our brother with someone so beautiful and sweet that we scared you. Please don't think we don't like you. At this point, we adore you. Possibly even more than our stupid brother."

Tavia waved me over, patting the couch beside her. "Join us," she said slowly.

Tentatively, I crossed the room and sat in the center of the couch. While Lexa took the other side of me, my gaze landed on the garbage bag at Tavia's feet. It was open, and I could see the dress I'd worn earlier sticking out of the top. I stiffened, my heart starting to pound again as I glanced around frantically for Max.

Following my gaze, Tavia quickly shook her head. "No, no," she said in a rush, pulling my gaze to her mouth. "It's not what you think. We stopped Max from burning these."

"What?" I signed, looking between the two women in

confusion. "Why would he burn my clothes? He spent so much money on them."

Lexa threw back her head in laughter. After a moment, she started fanning her face with her hand as tears of mirth spilled from her eyes. "Okay, okay. I'm good now," she signed, her lips moving as she spoke so Tavia could understand too. "It's just, it's obvious Max has kept a part of himself hidden from you, and that is absolutely adorable. My brother has never censored himself for anyone, but I'm seeing now that's because no one else has ever mattered."

"I don't understand," I told her honestly.

"Max is scared you're going to leave him, so he was going to burn your clothes to make it harder for you to run off." Lexa motioned toward the clothes. "Tavia saved them from becoming ashes."

"Thanks…?" Stunned, I was unsure of what else to say.

Lexa laughed again and grasped my hand, giving it a squeeze. "You are so different from Max's usual type." Jealousy hit me, and she seemed to see it because her next words were to reassure me. "That's a good thing, Delaney. You have nothing to worry about or be jealous over. Before you, Max didn't think about a girl past the first hour of meeting her. With you, he's ready to take on the world—or worse, our mom. And trust me, taking on Raven Reid is much scarier than taking on the entire world."

I gulped. "Your mom doesn't like me."

"That's where you're wrong." Her blue eyes softened. "Mom already loves you. The minute Max claimed you, she considered you hers. You can ask Tavia. When Raven claims you, she will move mountains to protect you. Things just got out of hand at the reception, and Mom didn't have time to welcome you to the family as she would have done under normal circumstances."

For some reason, I believed her. There was just something in her eyes that told me she was speaking the truth. Like with her brother, I sensed I could trust her. Earlier, when Max had tried to make excuses for how I'd felt everyone didn't want us to be together, I'd wanted to believe him then too. But I'd been so scared that he was trying to gloss over everything and didn't want to face the reality that his family didn't like me, that I couldn't allow myself to believe him.

Having it confirmed that he was right eased all my fears, and I was able to relax a little.

"Where is Max?" I asked, missing him.

"Our husbands needed a meeting with him," Lexa said. "They should be in the parking lot, but depending on what they have to do, they might have had to take a drive." She moved so she was sitting in the corner of the couch and folded her long legs under her. "Don't worry about him. Max can take care of himself. We want to know more about you."

"There isn't much to know," I signed with a shrug. "My parents died when I was young. I was sent to live with my aunt and uncle because there was no one else… At least, not that I knew of. Kelli… She came as a big surprise."

"For us too," Lexa agreed. "Kelli didn't grow up here like most of the people in our family. We all thought the only family she had left was River."

Curiosity got the better of me. "Can you tell me about her?"

"Kelli?"

I nodded.

"I don't know a lot about her past, but what I do know, most of the world does too. Kelli's dad was a senator here in California. He was dirty, and when her mom died, Kelli blamed him. To the point that she unleashed all his secrets.

The man went crazy because he lost everything. And he tried to kill her."

I wasn't sure what I was expecting to learn about my newfound aunt, but that was definitely not it. From what Kelli had told me earlier, her father would have been my grandfather. Realizing what the man was capable of—and trying to kill his own child, at that—made me grateful my mom had been adopted into a wonderful family that had showered her with love. That had taught her how to love in return.

"Kelli was shot in the chest," Lexa explained further. "Her dad died the same night, though. A heart attack or something like that. I don't really remember. I was only like five at the time. She married my uncle Colt not long afterward, and a year or so later, River was born."

"But what is she like?" I asked.

Lexa scratched her cheek without the scar on it for a moment before answering. "She's smart and mouthy at times. A bit of a hard-ass. She tells you how it is. Doesn't sugarcoat anything, for anyone—no exceptions. She always says it wastes too much time. But she can be incredibly kind, and when she loves you, she makes sure you know it."

I let all of that sink in, realizing I already liked the woman who was my last link to my mom. When I lost her, I'd thought I'd lost all connections with her. But discovering Kelli—and even River—renewed that connection for me. As hard as the day had been, it had also been a blessing.

Suddenly, I didn't feel so alone in the world.

For the next hour, Lexa and Tavia told me about themselves, with Lexa mostly translating for Tavia because the younger woman would get so animated that she would forget to talk slowly and I wouldn't be able to understand anything she said. I enjoyed getting to know them both, but I especially loved it when they talked about their babies. The love that shone from their eyes when Lexa mentioned Finn or Tavia told me about all of Rai's milestones seemed to light up the room, and I couldn't look away from either one of them when they did.

Both babies were with Raven, so they had the evening free to hang out with me. But I got the feeling she was the only person either of them trusted enough to babysit to enable them to be so at ease.

"I have to go back to New York tomorrow," Tavia said with a sad twist of her mouth. "We really only meant to stop in for the graduation and subsequent wedding, but when you showed up, and then Gian wanted to talk about your uncle, Theo decided to stay overnight."

"Wait, wait." I stopped her, my blood turning to ice with fear for the man I loved. "Are you saying that Max is meeting with your husbands to discuss Uncle Tony?"

Tavia's mouth closed, her gaze going over my shoulder to Lexa, as if asking how she should answer. Turning my head, I caught Lexa speaking behind my back. "...doesn't know," were the only words I read before she clamped her mouth shut.

"I don't know what?" I asked.

She kept her mouth closed, and I focused on Tavia. After spending a little time with them, I'd already realized Tavia was the sweeter of the two and possibly the easier to break if they were keeping secrets.

"What...don't...I know?" I spoke the words, hoping they were loud enough for her to hear.

"It's just that... Well, you think Max is so sweet and all..." Tavia's shoulders dropped. "And he can be. Don't get me wrong. I love him. But he's..."

I glanced quickly back and forth between the two sisters when she stopped speaking, trying to figure out what the heck I'd missed. "He's what?" I demanded, frustrated with them. "And what does that have to do with him meeting up with your husbands to talk about my evil uncle?" I jumped to my feet when neither responded to my signed question. "Don't you understand that he's in danger? Tony could hurt Max!"

Grimacing, Lexa waved me back down, urging me to sit. "Relax, sweetie. You have nothing to worry about. If anything, I would be more concerned for the safety of your awful uncle than my baby brother."

That she had so much confidence in her brother's ability wasn't reassuring at all. Max was too gentle and kind. She was out of her mind if she thought my uncle wouldn't tear him apart within seconds, despite how beast-like he was in appearance.

Without thinking about it, I ran to the door and flung it open. My only thought was to find Max and make sure he was safe.

His wide shoulders took up most of the stairs as he climbed them with two other men. Seeing me, he stopped, and his metallic-blue eyes turned hungry as he took in what I was wearing. Then his nostrils flared, and he sprinted up the last of the steps before pushing me back inside and slamming the door in the other two's faces. "Where do you think you're going dressed like that?" he demanded, his eyes trailing over me possessively.

"I was worried about you." I tried to explain.

"Go put some clothes on," he instructed, a muscle ticking in his clenched jaw. "Everything covered up."

I rolled my eyes at him. "I wore less than this to the reception." His shirt alone covered more of me than my dress had earlier.

"Don't remind me," he signed, his hands fisting. "I'm

trying really hard not to think about all those assholes getting to see so much of what is mine. Clothes. Now."

Glaring at him, I stomped over to where my bag of clothes was and carried it to our room. Pulling on a pair of jeans and a long-sleeved shirt, I gathered my hair into a pony-tail before walking barefoot back into the living room.

The two men who had been at the door with Max were now inside, but they hadn't taken a seat yet. The bigger one was covered in more ink than Max, his hair cut military-style. I knew from the pictures on the walls that he was Ben, Lexa's husband, and also the sheriff. The other guy, Theo, was leaner, his hair a little longer on top. He was married to Tavia, but just looking at him, I got the feeling he wasn't nearly as sweet as his wife.

Yet he was the first one to offer me a smile when I returned. Winking, he sat on the arm of the couch beside Tavia.

"I have to go out for the night," Max stated when my eyes landed on him. "I don't want you to be alone, so Lexa and Tavia are taking you to Lexa's house for a sleepover."

"No."

His eyes narrowed on me. "Yes."

"No," I repeated. "Because I know you're going to go confront my uncle. I'm not going to just sit here and wait for someone to tell me you got killed tonight!"

His smile softened his face, making him that much more beautiful. "That won't happen, treasure. We're just going to pay dear old Uncle Tony a small visit to make sure he under-stands that you have a new family now. So he won't be wasting his time in case he's still looking for you. I'll grab your things too, if you want. If there's anything you want that you had to leave behind, let me know, and I will make sure to bring it back."

"Take me with you," I countered.

"No," he signed with a shake of his head. "You are going to Lexa's."

"It will be so much fun," Lexa cut in, distracting me. "Nova is coming over too. And her cousin Ciana, who is visiting for the weekend with Tavia. We're going to make tacos and churros. We'll watch some rom-coms, or whatever you're in the mood for, and have some quality girl time."

She made it seem like so much fun, and I'd never actually been to a sleepover before. But as much as I wanted to go, I couldn't stomach the thought of Max coming face-to-face with Uncle Tony or his men. After giving him my heart, I couldn't imagine my life without him, and I was certain that my uncle wouldn't hesitate to hurt him.

Sensing my reluctance, Lexa smiled. "All of the men are going with him, Delaney. Including Ben. I seriously doubt anything bad will happen when he has an actual sheriff with him, do you?"

When she put it like that, I felt a little better. My uncle would think twice about doing anything bad if the cops showed up at his house. But I still couldn't shake the feeling of uneasiness. If anything happened to Max…

Max cupped the side of my face, tilting my head up to meet his gaze. "I'll be back before you even miss me."

"I already miss you."

"Treasure." He bent, pressing his forehead to mine for a moment. When he lifted his head, he stepped back, determination in his gaze. "You are going to Lexa's house. I will be back by morning."

20

MAX

Ben, Theo, and Gian stood in the garage parking lot. Since Gian and Theo had considered each other enemies this time the previous year, it was weird as fuck to see the two of them standing side by side. It was crazy how much could change in so little time.

But considering I'd met and fallen for my treasure in the blink of an eye, maybe it wasn't so crazy after all.

When I reached them, they didn't waste time getting to the point.

"Is your woman really the niece of Tony Garcia?" Gian asked, his face tight.

"He married Delaney's aunt," I explained. "There is no blood relation."

"The bastard is one of the biggest players in human trafficking this side of the country," he gritted out, the scar on his cheek seeming to pulse.

I'd been reluctant to welcome Gian when Monroe married him, but once Lexa made it clear she didn't hold him accountable for his father's sins, I'd begun to warm up to the asshole.

The man who had given him his scar was the one responsible for my sister's. Until the year before, we'd all assumed that man was Gian's father. DNA tests had proven that to be false. Now he was working to find out who his real father was.

But whether Enzo Fontana was his biological daddy or not, Gian was now in charge of Carlo Santino's empire. If anyone knew who the bigwigs in the underworld on this side of the country really were, it would be him.

"All of his whorehouses are filled with underage girls who have been snatched from across the Midwest. My sources tell me he's expanded up into Canada for fresh victims as well. The majority of them are in Mexico, but he has a few in Nevada that are legit enough in appearance on the outside. They're actually where he stashes the girls before he smuggles them down to Mexico." He glanced up at my apartment for a second before turning his gaze back on me. "If he let her make it to her eighteenth birthday without putting her to work, then he must have been saving her for something—or maybe even someone—huge."

My anger at the fucker began to boil all over again. There was no way in hell I was going to let Garcia hurt Delaney. I'd put a bullet in him before he even breathed the same air as her. "Like what?"

"Man, it could be anything. But if she was a virgin, then he could have gotten top dollar for it. He's been known to auction off the virgins. That movie *Taken* was pretty spot-on in some aspects. But he wouldn't have necessarily let her make it to eighteen before doing that. He thinks the younger they are, the better." He drifted into silence for a second, deep in thought, before shaking his head in frustration. "There are too many possibilities."

"Bash mentioned there was an issue a few days back."

Ben's knowing eyes drilled into me. "Said you and Spider had a talk with some newcomer and sent him on his way?"

"He was Garcia's man," was all I told him.

"Meaning he still wants Delaney for some reason," Gian concluded. "You need to deal with this guy now. Your woman won't be safe until he understands that she is no longer useful to him."

I'd planned on dealing with him all along. I had been waiting for the right time to take a trip south for it. Now it appeared I couldn't postpone the meeting with Delaney's uncle.

"We will go with you," Theo announced, having remained quiet, observing the entire conversation. "Between my men and Ryan's, we will have a small army with us."

"I don't need an army," I growled at him. Just me and a gun, that was all I really needed to take the motherfucker out.

"You will need one even to get close to Garcia's place. How that girl ran away without getting caught must have been a miracle of its own," Gian said with a trace of awe in his voice.

"She said the housekeeper helped her."

"Well, she's most likely dead now," he said with a lift of one shoulder. "I'll come with you as well."

"I'd rather take my brothers," I muttered. I might have accepted Fontana as family now, but that didn't mean I trusted him completely.

"If one of Garcia's men was in town, then he must have reported back that this place is run by the MC. He might know about me because I live here, but Garcia will be caught off guard to have Volkov and Vitucci forces showing up outside his place," Gian strategized. "He will piss his pants if they knock on his door. Everyone in the underworld knows that those two families run this entire country."

"Never thought I would say this," Theo grumbled. "But Fontana is right. Having a horde of MC roll up will just have them shooting. They will be expecting it if a spy was reporting back about what goes on in this town."

"Well, I'm not letting you fuckers go on your own," Ben said, crossing his bulky arms over his chest and glaring at us all. "Lexa will kill me if I let you three go in there and get your asses blown to hell. Plus, I'm the law. I can say we have a warrant or some shit and get us through the door faster. Any pants-pissing can come after we're through the gate."

"Sounds like a plan," Theo agreed. "The kids are at Raven's. Ryan can stay behind and watch over the women at your house."

It was easier than I expected to get Delaney to go to Lexa's for the night. Knowing she would be safe and happy with my sisters and with Ryan there to watch over them, I was able to focus on taking care of Garcia.

There was an iron fence around the house, with two guards standing in front of the gate. At a glance from the outside in, I understood what Gian meant about it being a miracle for Delaney to have gotten out without getting caught.

Delaney hadn't asked for me to bring back anything of hers, but she had wanted me to make sure Marta was okay. I had a feeling I wasn't going to get to fulfill that promise to my little treasure. Gian had been right about her getting out just in time, and I didn't doubt his conclusion about the housekeeper being dead. But if by some chance she was still breathing, then I promised myself before the gates even opened that I would bring her back to Creswell Springs with me.

She had saved Delaney, and I owed her for helping the

girl who owned my fucking soul survive long enough to get to me.

We were all stuffed into two of Ben's cruisers. When he pulled up to the gate, he had his lights on and brandished the fake warrant. The two guards spoke into their headsets, letting whoever was on the other end know what was going on, but they had little to no choice but to allow us through.

As we pulled up to the house itself, more guards came out. Ben slapped the warrant against some guy's chest, spouting some legal bullshit, while the rest of us were already climbing the steps to the front door. It wasn't until they saw that most of the men with us were wearing suits and I was in my cut that it became clear this was just a ploy to get inside.

But by the time their slow brains realized that, we were already in the house. I noticed immediately that there was no sign of anyone. No housekeeper. No Aunt June. And no fucking Tony.

Gian's gaze traveled over the other guards who were gathered in the foyer once we'd checked all the rooms in the house, his eyes narrowed as he took in each of their faces. "Where's Navarro?" he barked at the nearest man to him.

"Who?" I demanded.

"Navarro," he repeated. "Garcia's second-in-command. He's not here either."

The guard Gian had directed the question to remained mute. With a vicious curse, Gian grabbed the man by the throat. "Tell me where the fuck Navarro is." He didn't even flinch, and Gian pulled his gun, pressing it to the bastard's temple. "You have until the count of three to tell me before I put a bullet in your brain. One. Two. Th—"

"I don't know!" the guard cried, his voice shaking as he lost control of his composure. It just showed me that these fuckers knew exactly who Gian was, how ruthless and unforgiving he could be, but they'd had no clue how dangerous my MC brothers or I could really be. "He came back like two hours ago, and all he said was he was taking the boss to pick up the girl!"

My heart stopped, my feet suddenly glued to the spot as I watched the two of them.

"What's so fucking important about the girl?" Gian demanded.

"Boss has been promising her to his gun supplier. She was supposed to be his on her birthday or some shit. To cover his outstanding debt." Sweat poured down the guard's face. "When she ran, the supplier got pissed. Said he wanted what he was promised. Gave Boss until Monday to get her to him, or he threatened war. Navarro has been looking for her himself. When he got back, he took Boss and the supplier north." He gulped audibly. "Th-that's all I know, man. Honest."

"Fuck!" Ben and Theo muttered in unison behind me, but I barely heard them over the blood rushing through my ears.

Without a word to any of them, I took off like a bullet toward the cruiser. Too desperate to get to my girl, I didn't bother waiting for the others. I hopped into the driver's seat and started it up. But Ben, Theo, and two of his men jumped in before I could get it in gear. All I could think about was getting back to Creswell Springs as fast as I could.

My treasure was in danger.

I had to get to her.

21

DELANEY

Lexa's home was a two-story three-bedroom house in the same neighborhood as her parents, or so she told me as we stopped at the grocery store for all the ingredients for tacos and churros. By the time we were making tacos in the kitchen, Nova, Ryan, and his cousin Ciana arrived.

I hadn't seen Ciana at the reception, which I guess was understandable, considering everything that was going on. But then I took one look at her, and I wondered how I hadn't noticed her. She was gorgeous. Dark red hair that flowed down her back like glossy silk. Brown eyes that sat in a face that had the kind of beauty Grecian goddesses would have been jealous of.

The clothes she wore had designer labels on them, and her makeup looked like it had been expertly applied. When I first saw her walking through the kitchen door, I'd had this picture in my head of every mean girl who ever existed. And then she smiled so brightly at me when Nova introduced us and welcomed me with a hug.

She didn't know more than how to say "Hello" in ASL, but she talked slowly enough for me to understand her. Some people who had to speak slower when they addressed me made me feel like I was stupid, but Ciana didn't give off that vibe.

While we ate tacos in the kitchen, she told me about her life back in New York. She lived with her parents, was the middle sibling of five, and was going to college to be a nurse. Ryan made a face when she mentioned that little detail, making her shoot her cousin a glare. I wondered why he didn't like the thought of her being a nurse, but I didn't want to upset anyone by asking in case it was a touchy subject for either of them.

At first, I was confused about their family connection. Ciana was Ryan's cousin, but also Nova's. Yet Ryan and Nova weren't cousins. They weren't related at all. Nova explained to me that her mom was related to Ciana's dad, and Ryan's dad was Ciana's mom's older brother.

Lexa taught me how to make churros, which I'd always loved, and we ate them with vanilla ice cream, drizzled in caramel and chocolate sauce. Time flew by in the blink of an eye, and before I realized it, over three hours had passed since Max had left me.

I missed him like crazy, but I had to admit I was having fun with his sisters and extended family.

I thought it was an all-girls' sleepover, so when Ryan changed into a pair of sweats and dropped down onto the couch beside Nova, who was in her pajamas like the rest of us were to watch the movie I'd picked, it surprised me. I didn't know if sleepovers were typically co-ed or not, so I didn't bring it up as we settled in to watch *Pirates of the Caribbean*.

I'd watched the movie with my parents many times, and it was one of my favorites, but I hadn't gotten the chance to see it in years. Lexa turned on the subtitles for me and passed out bowls of popcorn as the opening scene rolled.

The lights were off, with just the glow of the television to see by. My focus was completely on the screen, trying to take in the scene of Jack Sparrow fighting with William Turner while reading the captions at the bottom of the screen. I didn't do this often, mostly because it was kind of exhausting. I missed a good portion of the movie because I was either reading what they were saying or watching the scene itself play out.

It was why I'd rather read a book than watch TV, but as far as I knew, reading wasn't exactly a sleepover activity.

Nova was sitting beside me, and Ryan suddenly jerked her up and behind him as he jumped to his feet, pulling a handgun from what seemed like thin air because I hadn't noticed him packing one earlier. Shocked at the sudden movement, I glanced around, trying to make sense of what was going on.

The lights clicked on, making it easier to see, and I immediately wanted them to be switched off again. The front door was hanging off its hinges, Uncle Tony and his second-in-command standing there with their own guns drawn, pointing them straight at Ryan, who was the only threat to them I could see. Ryan held the gun with confidence, as if it had been attached to his hand from birth. It didn't shake, didn't so much as waver as he sneered something at my uncle and Navarro.

Lexa and Tavia, who had been on the opposite side of the living room, stood together, their mouths moving too rapidly for me to make out what they were saying. Meanwhile, Ciana sat on the couch, still eating her popcorn and watching the reality scene play out with more interest than the one currently playing on the flat-screen.

I took it all in within a few seconds before swiveling my

head back to Uncle Tony, too afraid to let him out of my line of sight for long.

"No one said Vitucci would be here!" I thought Uncle Tony said, his face drawing into tight lines as he kept his gaze on Ryan. "What the fuck? How did we not know this was their territory?"

Navarro didn't answer. As long as I'd known him, I'd rarely seen him speak much. If I hadn't witnessed it on a few occasions, I would have thought he didn't even possess a tongue. His dark eyes were trained on Ryan like a laser, his gun pointed directly at Ryan's heart.

"We just want my niece," Uncle Tony said, his face covered in sweat as he took a hesitant step toward me. "Let me have her, and no one has to get hurt."

I gulped, my terror so strong I could taste bile rising into the back of my throat. Tears filled my eyes, and I got slowly to my feet. I didn't know if Ryan or Lexa were saying anything, but I knew I couldn't let them be in danger if I could do anything about it.

A strong hand grasped my wrist, and I was suddenly behind Ryan. Nova tugged me closer to her, her hands moving quickly as she told me everything was going to be okay.

I shook my head. "No. I have to go with them. He will kill everyone. I won't let them hurt you and your family," I signed.

"You have to trust me, Delaney," she replied, her eyes hard. "They don't know who they are dealing with. Ryan will take care of this until Max and Ben get here."

My frustration pushed down some of my fear. These people were delusional. They had no idea how dangerous my uncle was. I'd only seen a fraction of what he was capable of from my bedroom window, but I'd known there were worse things happening in the house. I couldn't stomach the thought of something happening to any of these people I'd already come to care about.

Pushing Nova's hands off my arms, I moved around Ryan, who still had his gun aimed at the door.

Uncle Tony and Navarro were no longer the only ones standing in the doorway. A man I'd only caught a glimpse of a few times was standing there. As with every time I'd spotted him from my bedroom window in the past, my heart started pounding in sheer terror at the sight of him.

He wore an expensive suit that bulged out at the sides, making me think he was hiding more than one gun beneath his jacket. His hair was liberally sprinkled with gray, but his face suggested he was younger than his salt-and-pepper hair let on. He was shorter than either Uncle Tony or Navarro, but there was something about the way he stood between the two men that made him look larger-than-life.

His eyes, dark like a moonless night, zeroed on me, and I saw something flash in their depths that caused my stomach to churn. The same hunger Max got in his eyes when he looked at me was there in this man's.

"It's time to go, Delaney," he spoke slowly so I could understand him. "Come with me willingly, and I will leave your new friends unharmed. Force my hand, and I will take every one of their lives."

L exa

I had a feeling of déjà vu as I watched Delaney take a step toward the fucker who wanted to take her. Memories flooded me of the night Carlo Santino had tried to take me for his adopted son, Gian—when I'd had to make the same choice.

Cower like a scared little girl behind Ben, or give in and protect the people I loved by going with the enemy.

Really, there was no choice to make. I understood it, but I hated that she felt she had to make it, especially when I knew there was no need.

Ben had called me as soon as he and my brother learned that Tony Garcia was possibly on his way to take back his niece. Not two minutes after I got the call from my husband, Dad texted me to let me know that he not only had MC brothers watching the house, but Trigger would have his sniper rifle pointed at my living room.

I'd shown Tavia the texts from Dad just as Ryan's phone had gotten an alert. While he'd been busy with his phone, I excused myself, not wanting to freak out the newest member of my family, and grabbed one of Ben's extra guns from the safe in our bedroom. After I stuffed it into the back of my pajama pants, I'd returned to my guests and went on about the evening like nothing was wrong.

Seeing the stark fear on Delaney's face made me wish I'd taken the time to explain a few things to her about our family. But Max had been so worried that he would lose her if she found out what his life was really like. I hadn't liked that he was hiding a part of himself, was convinced he was worrying for no reason. I'd seen firsthand the way his special little treasure looked at him, not only at River's wedding reception but later at his apartment.

I knew that look all too well. I lived that look every time my gaze landed on my husband.

Delaney loved Max. I didn't need her to speak or sign those words for me to know she was completely head over heels for my baby brother.

Which meant that she was now my sister, just as much as

Tavia was. And I would gladly give up my life for either of them.

When my front door crashed open, the wood practically splitting down the middle under the pressure of the dumb fuck who decided to kick it down, I barely flinched. Ben had texted me only minutes before, alerting me to the fact that they had just gotten to Creswell Springs. Knowing he was so close, I refrained from drawing my own gun, wanting to save that element of surprise in case we needed it, should Ben and Max not arrive in time.

The three idiots who stepped into my house were about to have the worst—and last—day of their miserable lives.

Delaney

I hesitated for only a second before taking a step in his direction. But as I did, I saw movement behind the man. I didn't have time to react as Max lifted a gun and placed it to the back of the man's skull. Before I could blink, he fell on his face, while blood seeped into Lexa's carpet.

My eyes didn't stay on the dead man long. Lifting my gaze back to Max, I was just in time to see him turn the gun on Navarro, and he pumped his trigger finger twice, putting a bullet in the man's chest and then his head.

He moved like lightning, popping my uncle in the head so quickly, I barely had time to take it in before the floor was littered with dead bodies. And all at the hands of the man I loved.

The whole thing took less than five seconds. Not giving Uncle Tony or Navarro time to react or defend themselves before they were dead at Max's feet. If I had blinked, I was sure I would have missed the entire incident and would have questioned who was responsible for their deaths. Even though

I'd watched everything as it happened as if it were a movie played in super-slow motion, I still wasn't completely sure I'd actually seen what I had.

Dropping his hand that still held the gun, he turned those metallic blues on me, his chest heaving with each breath he took as the house filled with other people, all of them with their guns drawn. Ben, then Theo, and several men I didn't recognize in suits were shouting, from what I could tell with how their mouths were moving, but I barely paid them any attention as I kept my focus on Max.

He'd killed all three of those men like it was nothing. He hadn't flinched, hadn't even hesitated as he pulled the trigger over and over again with such confidence, I knew he'd killed before.

I'd thought my Max was sweet and kind, gentle.

Now, I saw that he had been hiding a totally different side of himself. One that I couldn't wrap my head around.

There was blood on his face from where he'd blown not one, but three men's brains out. It made his face look wilder, almost feral, as he stepped toward me. Reflexively, I took a step back, unable to fully accept what I'd just witnessed firsthand.

Had I been blind during the entire time I'd known Max?

Or was he just that good at hiding this part of himself?

And more importantly…

Why wasn't I even a little scared of him now that I knew what he was capable of?

22

MAX

I COULDN'T FUCKING BREATHE.

The drive back to Creswell Springs had taken half the time with how fast I drove, but it felt like it took forever. During the drive, Ben called ahead, telling Lexa to be ready in case someone showed up to take Delaney. Once my sister knew the possible danger, he'd called Dad, and they were supposed to watch the house, but from a distance.

They knew I wanted to deal with Garcia myself. Dad promised he wouldn't intervene unless they tried to take Delaney or someone started shooting. I knew my sister and Ryan would protect those in the house if it came down to it, but just the idea of Delaney being in harm's way was enough to steal the air from my chest.

Putting an end to whoever the fuck the supplier was, then the guy I suspected was Navarro, and finally, the fucker who was supposed to protect my treasure for all those years but never had, gave me an all-too-brief moment of satisfaction. And then I took one look at Delaney, realized what I'd just shown her about myself, and knew from the expression on her beautiful face that it was very possible I could still lose her.

I took one step toward her, and she backed away, practically cowering against Ryan as he steadied her.

My heart lifted into my throat, choking me as I took a chance and held out my free hand to her.

She looked down at it, then at the one still holding the gun that only moments before had fired the bullets that took the lives of three men right in front of her. Her forehead wrinkled with how tight her brows pinched together, as if she didn't know what to do.

I didn't breathe—*couldn't* fucking breathe—as I waited to see if she would take my hand. I'd never wanted her to know about this part of me, and there was no way of hiding it or even taking it back now. Not when some motherfucker had been there to snatch her away from me. I would have done it again, over and over, if it meant she was safe and still standing there where she belonged.

Not where she belonged, I reminded myself.

Where she truly belonged was in my arms, and she had yet to move so much as an inch in my direction.

But then she inhaled sharply and launched herself at me. I dropped the gun, catching her with both hands as she locked her legs around my waist and wrapped her arms around my neck. I was finally able to draw in a deep enough breath, and I sucked in one lungful after another, filling my senses with her sweet scent as she sobbed into my neck.

"Max," she cried my name, her small body trembling.

I rocked her in my arms, trying to reassure myself that she was safe now. Garcia was no longer a threat. No one was ever going to try to take her from me again.

While I held my treasure, everyone else was moving around quickly, already cleaning up the mess I'd made.

Behind me, the flashing lights of other cop cruisers filled the driveway. Smartly, Dad and the rest of my MC brothers stayed in the shadows of wherever they were positioned, keeping watch over my sister's house. Ben spoke to one of his deputies, telling him whatever story he had come up with to explain away the dead bodies at my feet.

It wasn't the first time he'd had to come up with something on the fly to cover for a dead body I was responsible for. And given that the dead men were all known felons, the deputies didn't really look too hard to see if what their boss told them was the truth or not.

Lexa walked over to me, untucking the Glock she must have stuffed into the back of her pajama bottoms when Ben had called her earlier. Handing it to her husband, she kissed him long and hard before touching her hand to Delaney's back.

When my girl lifted her head, Lexa gave her a small smile. "You okay?" she signed.

Delaney paused for a moment before nodding.

"Good," my sister said with a sigh. "I was scared I was going to have to put a bullet in those bozos myself if Max hadn't gotten here in time. You were going to go with these creeps to save us, but sweetheart, you need to understand that we never would have let anything happen to you or anyone else. You are one of us now. Understand?"

"I'm starting to," Delaney responded, releasing her hold on my neck, trusting me to hold on to her as she signed. "Maybe if someone had let me know what he was really like, I wouldn't have questioned everyone's sanity around here. I mean, I thought you were all just these sweet but kind of gullible idiots for thinking you could take on Uncle Tony. I had no clue you were all badasses with your own arsenal."

Smirking, Lexa winked at me. "I guess someone thought he would scare you off if you knew the truth."

I glared at her, but I kept my mouth shut. She wasn't wrong, so I didn't have a good enough defense to fire back at her.

Delaney's soft fingers trailed over the back of my neck soothingly. I leaned into her touch, needing it more than anything else right then. "Maybe he would have," she signed after a moment, her eyes caressing over my face. "If he hadn't shown me the softer side of himself first."

Having her reassurance that I hadn't scared her off eased a little more of my tension. I didn't know what I would have done if she hadn't wanted anything more to do with me after seeing what I was capable of, but I knew my world would have been dark without her.

It took a while to get everything sorted out. Once the coroner showed up to take the bodies away, Dad gave the okay to clean up the mess I'd made of Lexa's carpet. Reid must have been on standby because he brought in a crew, took up the carpet and laid out a new one in the living room in under an hour before replacing the door.

Lexa frowned down at the new color. "I guess it will do," she said with a grimace. "Maybe keep a few other color selections on hand for the future, though, cuz."

"You take what you get and don't throw a fit," Dad told her as he watched the room slowly empty of the construction crew before turning his gaze on Delaney. She was still in my arms. There had been no attempt by her to make me put her down, and I was all too happy to carry her around for the rest of forever if she wanted me to. "Spider went over to check out the garage. Bastards wrecked your apartment, broke the front window of the shop, and bent in the doors of half the garage bays. Your mom wants you to stay at the house tonight."

I knew better than to think it was a request. If I didn't take Delaney over there tonight, I knew Mom would come looking for us. Giving my dad a simple nod to let him know we would be there, I reluctantly placed my girl on her feet. "Treasure, go get the things you brought with you."

She leaned into me for a moment, and I kissed the top of her head. Giving me a tiny smile, she bounced up the stairs to get the overnight bag she'd packed for herself earlier to spend the night with my sister.

"See you at home," Dad said after saying his goodbyes to my sisters.

Ryan, Nova, and Ciana had left after the deputies had, and they were at my parents' house when we got there twenty minutes later. Lexa, Tavia, and Delaney had taken forever to say their goodbyes. I was glad the three of them were becoming friends, but it was three in the morning and I was about to crash. I just needed a bed and my treasure so I could sleep.

But as soon as we walked into the house, Mom was all over Delaney, making sure she was okay. With wide eyes, Delaney allowed herself to be mothered. Only after Mom had made sure Delaney was perfectly fine did she turn her attention on me. But she knew me. She understood that I needed her to comfort Delaney in every possible way more than I needed anything else from her.

"Are you hungry?" She was already shoving a plate of sandwiches into my hands. Her voice wasn't soft, as it had been with my girl—not that Delaney would have known that —but harder, her normal tone whenever she spoke to me. Mom didn't do soft and sweet often, and rarely with me. But that just showed me even more how much she loved me. "Eat this before you fall into a coma, kiddo. Who knows how long you will be out after the adrenaline of the day finally deserts you?"

She was right. I was running on fumes. I inhaled the food, then scooped up Delaney and carried her up to my childhood bedroom. Kicking off my boots, I stripped to my boxer briefs before going into the bathroom to wash my face. When I returned, Delaney had the covers pulled back and was sitting in the middle of the bed.

Fuck, but I couldn't remember seeing a more beautiful sight. Her hair was hanging over one shoulder as she sat cross-legged with her back against the headboard. I could see the tiredness in her eyes, but she patted the bed beside her and gave me a smile that was so bright, it warmed all the cold places that had lingered.

I face-planted beside her, and she instantly started stroking her fingertips up and down my back. In no time, I was out.

23

DELANEY

MAX WAS STILL ASLEEP WHEN I LEFT HIS OLD BEDROOM THE next morning. Pulling my hair up into a ponytail, I walked into the kitchen to find it crowded with people, some I knew, some I couldn't remember meeting.

As soon as they spotted me, Nova and Ciana threw their arms around me.

"How are you feeling?" Nova asked.

"I'm okay," I told her with a small smile, before glancing around shyly at the others.

She tugged me forward. "Come meet the others."

I was introduced to Ciana's parents, Ciro and Scarlett, as well as her younger brothers, Vito and Benito. Both were named after their grandfathers and were identical twins. They were about the same age as Nova, from what I garnered, but the two of them looked years older than she was.

I'd met Nova's parents, Felicity and Jet, the night before when Max and I had first arrived. Her brother, Garret, was seated at the huge kitchen table with everyone else, but other than giving me a brief appraisal and a single nod in greeting, he'd mostly sat there eating his breakfast. It wasn't hard to see the differences in the two siblings. They looked a lot alike in appearance, but their personalities were as different as night and day.

Nova was sweet sunshine with a dash of sassy and feistiness, while her brother was a moody asshole. Making a mental note to avoid him as much as possible, I let Nova push me into a chair at the table on the opposite end from Garret.

Raven placed a plate of eggs, bacon, and home fries in front of me. I thanked her, and she gently ran a single finger down my cheek. The action was one my own mom used to make, bringing tears to my eyes that I had to quickly blink away.

The night before, I'd been blown away by how she'd so readily welcomed me. Considering I was responsible for her son killing three men at point-blank range, I'd thought she would be angry with me, but she was more concerned about me than she seemed to be about Max. I no longer had the feeling that she disapproved of me being with her son.

As Lexa had said, her mom seemed to already consider me part of their family.

Someone placed a glass of juice in front of me, and I spent the next half hour eating and getting to know the others at the table. They all seemed intrigued and maybe even a little fascinated by me. By the time our plates were empty, everyone who had no ASL knowledge had a few signs down. Having them want to learn to communicate with me warmed my heart.

Not long after the kitchen was cleaned up from our huge meal, Nova started saying her goodbyes, while the other guests gathered their luggage. Nova and her brother spent the summers with their family in New York City, and she was flying back with them.

I was sad to see one of my newest and closest friends go,

but I knew she would be back before school started once again.

At the front door, she threw her arms around me, giving me a tight hug. "I'll text you every day," she promised when she pulled back. "If you need anything, just let me know. I might be in another state, but I can light a fire under people if I need to."

After she stepped back, Ciana gave me a hug, and we exchanged numbers. "By the way," she said slowly, her eyes bright with amusement. "Last night was the most fun I've had in forever. Seriously, best 'sleepover' ever."

"You are so weird," Nova said, signing so I could understand. "Don't listen to her, Delaney. She gets plenty of excitement back at home."

Grinning, I waved to them as they walked down the driveway to where two limos were waiting for them. Ryan was already standing at the back door of one, and Nova practically bounced toward him. He gave me a brief wave before urging Nova inside and following her.

As I watched, Garret rolled two suitcases toward the second limo, his dad carrying a box behind them. It looked like he was planning on staying longer than Nova from how much stuff he was taking with him.

"Garret isn't coming back," Raven signed when she caught me frowning after her nephew. "He hates the small-town life. Boy was committed to getting out as fast as he possibly could."

She didn't look the least bit sad that he wasn't planning on returning, making me wonder just what kind of trouble Garret had gotten into over the years.

I glanced back at him to find his mom was now standing by the trunk of the second limo. She'd been so nice earlier, her face practically glowing. Now, it was pulled into a hard glare as she stood in front of her son. She pointed a finger up at him, her mouth moving, but I was unable to make out what she said since I could only see half of her face. Whatever she said, however, had Garret's jaw clenching.

When she was done speaking, she gave him a brief hug and stepped back. Jet gave him a longer hug, slapped his son on the back, then walked over to the other limo to peek inside. Felicity's face softened as she spoke to those in the first limo, which held Ryan, Nova, and Ciana.

When they stepped back from the limo, Jet closed the door, and the driver pulled away. I'd learned over breakfast that Tavia and Lexa had arrived before I'd woken to retrieve their babies and so Tavia could say goodbye to Raven. I wasn't sure how the other woman had become Raven's "daughter," but I hoped one of them would tell me the story one day. From what little I'd seen of them so far, I could tell their relationship was almost as close as Lexa and Raven's was.

Max's mom put her hand on my shoulder and nodded toward the door. "You should wake Max. We need to clean up your place, and Bash is going to need his help fixing the garage bay doors."

Upstairs, I stepped into Max's room. The sun was shining through the window, filling the room with natural light so I could easily see to get to the bed. Max had shifted in his sleep and was now lying on his stomach with one arm wrapped tightly around my pillow. That was typically how we slept, and the sight made my heart melt. Even in his sleep, he needed to have me close.

Even though he hadn't told me he loved me yet, I knew he did. There was no way he could treat me the way he did, protect me so fearlessly, and not love me as much as I loved him.

I just wished he would say the words already.

Of course, it was too soon, but dang it, I wanted them.

Pushing those thoughts away, I smiled to myself as I climbed onto the bed and straddled his hips. After rubbing my hands together to warm them, I started rubbing them up and down his back with gentle pressure.

The vibrations under my fingertips told me he was groaning in pleasure. Once again, the need to hear him was almost overwhelming. If I could have one wish, only one, it would be to hear Max. Biting my lip to keep it from trembling, I added a little more pressure, working on the knots in his tight muscles.

I massaged him for several minutes, simply enjoying making him feel good. But then he shifted, one arm reaching behind him to hold my waist as he rolled over beneath me while keeping me firmly in place. Only now, I was straddling his hips, and his very hard erection was pressed deliciously against my core, with only his boxer briefs and my shorts and panties between us.

"You are so damn beautiful," he signed, his eyes drifting over me like a physical touch. "I could lie here for the rest of my life just looking up at you like this, treasure."

"But we have work to do," I reminded him. "We need to clean up the apartment, and Raven said you need to help your dad with the damage done to the garage." Remorse filled me, and I swallowed the lump that filled my throat. "I'm so sorry they did that to the garage."

"Don't be. It wasn't your fault, baby." Sitting up with me still on his lap, he kissed the tip of my nose. "I don't want you worrying about it or anything else. Reid and his construction crews will come in and help us fix or replace anything we have to. I promise you, it's no big deal. It just might take us a day or two to get things back to the way they were."

My nod of acceptance was all he needed before he rolled me beneath him. He kissed me long and slow, making love to my mouth but never once touching the rest of my body. When he pulled back, he signed, "I want you so bad, treasure. But I can't fuck you here. You're so loud, I know the entire house will hear us, if not the neighbors."

Heat filled my cheeks. I had no idea I was loud during sex. He'd never said anything about it, and I hadn't thought to ask. Noise wasn't something I regularly considered because it was completely absent from my life.

"Tonight, we will be back in our own bed, and I'll make you scream over and over," he promised with a wicked look shining out of his metallic eyes. "Don't plan on getting any sleep tonight."

I pressed my thighs together in anticipation. "Let's go clean up the apartment now, then," I signed excitedly. "Because I need you."

Grinning, Max stood and then lifted me from the bed, placing me on my feet. Slapping me on the ass, he nudged me toward the door. "Let Mom know I'll be down after a quick shower. If you two want to head on over, I'll grab a ride with Dad. I'm not sure what shape the Tahoe is in, but I'll worry about that later."

I didn't want to go without him, but getting our home cleaned up as quickly as possible so we could have our privacy was my top priority. I practically skipped downstairs to let Raven know what he'd said. As if she'd known that would be his decision, she was standing by the back door with her keys already in hand.

Laughing, I followed her out to her own Tahoe and got in the passenger seat.

24

DELANEY

The damage done to the garage was noticeable as soon as Raven pulled into the parking lot. The shop's huge front window was completely shattered, and from the looks of it, things had been thrown everywhere inside. My heart felt heavy as we passed the garage bays and I saw just how beat-up they were. It looked like someone had rammed their vehicle into two of the doors. The other damaged doors weren't nearly as bad, but still hard to look at.

If Uncle Tony, Navarro, and the man who had come to take me away the night before had caused this much property damage, just how much destruction would they have caused in human lives? I shivered at the possibilities. I could have so easily lost everyone in that house the night before, and it left me feeling sick to my stomach just imagining it.

The damage downstairs was nothing to that in the actual apartment. The door had been kicked in, the thick wood splintered in the middle, and the door hung off its hinges. The couch had been turned upside down. All the pictures on the walls were now on the floor, the majority of which were broken, the glass littering the living room floor.

In the kitchen, dishes were broken all over the place, the fridge was lying on its front and unplugged, making all the food inside inedible.

The bedroom was the worst, though. They had taken a knife to the pillows and the mattress itself, and everything from the closet was scattered on the floor. At first glance, it didn't look like any of my stuff was missing, until I started picking up my clothes and realized my panties and bras were nowhere to be found.

"Gross," I signed to Raven. "That guy always gave me the creeps when I would see him from my bedroom window back at Aunt June's house. But I didn't realize he was…"

"Obsessed with you?" she offered when I couldn't find the words to describe him. I nodded. "It can happen with something as simple as a glance," she explained with a twist of her mouth. "Maybe he saw you staring at him when you were looking out your window and imagined you were just as emotionally invested as he was."

"I'm just glad he's gone now," I told her before picking up a pair of Max's jeans and folding them.

"Me too, sweet girl."

The two of us worked together and attacked one room at a time, starting with the living room. Some of the pictures that had Max in them had been ripped in half, but Raven promised me it wouldn't be any trouble replacing them. All she had to do was print most of them off her computer at home.

Everything in the kitchen had to be trashed. Raven told me that once we got the place cleaned up, the two of us would go shopping for new everything—dishes, fridge, and mattress, especially.

By the time we were finished with the kitchen, Max and his dad came upstairs to let us know they were going to the hardware store for a few parts. He told me his cousin hadn't arrived yet but should be by with a new window for the shop before he returned.

Giving me a kiss, he made sure I didn't need anything before following his dad out the door.

Between moving around heavy furniture and lifting all the trash bags we kept filling, my body was beginning to feel the effects, causing me to move slower as we started the cleanup of the bedroom. Raven was cleaning up the pillow and mattress stuffing with a shop-vac, and I was closer to the door, picking up the clothes and folding them as I piled them up next to me on the floor.

When a hand caught my ponytail, jerking my head back, I cried out so hard, I felt a sting in my throat. Startled by the sudden attack, I didn't have time to react when I was forced to my feet and had something cold and hard pressed to my temple.

R aven
The dull ache in my back from having to clean up the mess caused by Garcia and his men was enough to make me fantasize about being the one to take the bastards out. My son popping them a few times with a bullet wasn't nearly enough punishment in my eyes.

With the destruction they had caused, the fear they had put my newest daughter through, and the danger they had put other members of my family in, I wanted to make it long and painful. Poor Delaney was taking it all in stride, thankfully. Max hiding the darker side of our lives from her had been wrong on so many levels, but after she'd passed my first test —making sure it was love she was feeling and not something more nefarious—I hadn't been worried that she would run screaming and crying in the other direction when Max's true self was unveiled to her.

A noise caught my attention, and I turned to check on Delaney out of instinct. When my gaze landed on her standing there, a woman I knew from pictures to be her bitch Aunt June, who was supposed to have taken care of her the past eight years, pressing a gun to my newest daughter's head, I had to stiffen my muscles so I didn't immediately react.

Back when I'd gone with Kelli to look for Delaney, we'd learned a lot about Tony Garcia, but I had been more curious about the man's wife. She'd been given sole responsibility for her brother's daughter upon his death, and yet as many times as she'd been in gossip rags and other shit, never once was there a mention of her niece.

But those gossip rags and speaking to people who supposedly knew "the real June Garcia" had left me with the impression that June was possibly more dangerous than her vile husband.

After the fiasco of the night before, Bash had some of the MC brothers watching the house. A good thing, or they would have missed the men who had come with Garcia and Favre—the fucking French arms dealer himself, from what Lexa had told me when she and Tavia had picked up the kids that morning—and had been in hiding nearby. Ready to shoot the place up if and when bullets started flying.

Bash and the boys had taken them all out before they could cause trouble and hurt someone.

But they hadn't mentioned June. And I hadn't given the cunt much thought either.

I fucking should have, though.

"Tell me where Tony is!" June yelled, her hold on Delaney tightening.

I didn't answer, knowing if I so much as opened my mouth with how pissed I was at this bitch already, I would say something that would put Delaney in even more danger.

My silence only made June angrier, though, and she started spewing her hate-filled bullshit. The way she called Delaney names, making fun of her, making it seem like she was stupid and worthless, made my blood boil. But I still remained quiet. My body locked as I told Delaney with my eyes to stay strong, not to be scared. I would figure out some way to get rid of this monster from her past and keep her safe.

Bash and Max had been gone a while. One of them would come upstairs when they returned. Or Reid would when he arrived...

Just as the thought of them filtered through my head, movement behind June caught my attention.

Kelli.

She hadn't known about what went down the night before. After the wedding reception, Colt had said he was taking her home, and from the look in my brother's eyes, I didn't want to know what kind of kink they were going to get into. Bash had known about their plans too and hadn't bothered them when he got the call about trouble. But I'd called my sister-in-law that morning to let her know what had happened, not wanting her to hear it from a third party.

I'd invited her over to help clean up the apartment, knowing she would appreciate the opportunity to spend time with her newfound family member. Noting the knives she must have picked up in the kitchen, I was eternally grateful for the forethought of calling her.

· · ·

D elaney
Across the room, Raven stood motionless, her gaze locked with mine. I swallowed my fear, taking courage in the way she was looking at me, as if willing me not to freak out. I had no idea who held me, but I could feel from how they were pressed to my back that the person wasn't large. I inhaled slowly, both trying to calm my racing heart-beat and to take in my captor's scent.

When it hit my senses, I felt tears sting my eyes.

I would know that perfume anywhere. It was Aunt June's expensive and overwhelming fragrance. The few times I'd been in the same room with her over the years, I was left with a headache because of how overpowering that aroma was to me.

From the vibrations against my back, I could tell she was screaming, but still, Raven didn't react. She stood there, not even blinking at my aunt, her focus only on me and trying to reassure me that it was all going to be okay with just her eyes.

The inability to hear had never been more frustrating than in that moment. I had no idea what my aunt was saying. With my back to her and the gun to my head, I was powerless to know what was happening behind me and was completely unaware of what might happen next. But I forced myself to keep my eyes on Raven, to take my cues from her just in case.

A flicker of her lashes. It was barely a movement at all and one I was still questioning, but that was the only warning I had before I was suddenly propelled forward.

Breathing hard, I turned to find Kelli standing over Aunt June, who was facedown on the floor with a butcher knife sticking out of her back. Another knife was still in Kelli's hands as she glared down at the woman who was supposed to take care of me for the past eight years.

Raven was already picking up the gun my aunt had dropped. Rushing forward, she kicked Aunt June in the ribs, but the woman didn't move. Bending, Raven checked for a pulse then shook her head as she stood.

Oddly enough, I wasn't the least bit sad that my dad's sister was dead. If anything, the knot of anxiety that had lingered since the night before unraveled, and I was finally able to take a deep breath.

Kelli stepped over Aunt June's body like she was nothing more than unpleasant trash. Cupping my face, she spoke slowly. "Are you okay, honey?"

I gave a ready nod. "Th-thank you," I spoke aloud.

Her tense face softened. "No thanks needed, sweetheart. The bitch had it coming." Her arms wrapped around me in a tight hug just as the door filled up with Bash and Reid. But they were both pushed aside when I spotted Max's head over Kelli's shoulder.

His chest rose and fell in rapid, hard breaths. That wild, feral look was back in his eyes, but it didn't scare me. If anything, it calmed the fear that was still through me like a runaway train. Smartly, Kelli stepped back before he reached me only seconds later, and he lifted me into his arms. His entire body seemed to tremble as he molded my body to his own, his hands running over me in an attempt to reassure himself that I was unharmed.

Pulling back, he cupped each side of my face. "Are you okay?" he demanded, so upset he couldn't sign, but I read his lips easily.

I nodded, the rest of my fear fading away completely now that I was in his arms.

His thumbs tucked under my chin, making sure I was

looking right at him, but there was no need. All I saw was him. "I love you," he spoke each word slowly, making sure I understood each one of them, while his wild eyes stared into mine. "I love you, treasure. So fucking much."

"I-I love you too," I whispered—or at least I thought I did. But no matter how loud I spoke, I knew by the flare of his nostrils and the way his eyes darkened that he heard me.

Max pulled my head to his chest, kissing my hair, the side of my face, and down to my neck over and over again. I could feel how hard his heart was pounding against his ribs, and I pressed my palm into it, wanting to soothe the poor organ and wipe away his fear.

He hadn't even been like this the night before. He'd killed three men like it was nothing. But I'd learned afterward that he'd had the whole thing under control even though he hadn't been there at first. There had been men and guns on Lexa's house the entire time, and I'd realized I wasn't in nearly as much danger as I'd first thought.

But this time, Aunt June had come out of nowhere. There was no warning, no plan of action. If Kelli hadn't come over when she did, I didn't even know what might have happened.

Max and I stood like that for the longest time before his attention was pulled to everyone else in the room. Keeping one arm around me, he shifted us so we were facing the others. No one was signing, so I knew they didn't want me to know what was going on, but I could read their lips for the most part and got the gist of what they were talking about.

They debated whether to call Ben and decided against it. Bash and Reid assured the others they would take care of the body, and then Reid and Max would clean up and replace the carpet themselves to hide the proof of Aunt June ever being there. The entire time, it felt like they were discussing her like she was nothing more than extra trash that needed to be cleaned up in the mess that was our apartment, like the ruined mattress that was leaning against the wall to be hauled away.

I honestly didn't want to know how they were going to get rid of her body, any more than I cared about them hiding everything from the sheriff. I wasn't going to tell anyone a single thing about what had transpired there that day. For one, I wanted to forget all about the nightmare of both Uncle Tony and Aunt June. For another, I didn't want to chance anyone getting in trouble, especially not Kelli, who had saved me.

Raven and Kelli tugged me away from Max and into the living room. Reluctantly, he allowed me to leave him, telling me for the second time he loved me. Raven suggested we get something sweet to eat to combat the shock of what had happened, and then the three of us would go shopping for all the stuff we needed for the apartment.

Just like that, we were putting what had happened behind us, and truthfully, I was kind of relieved. I didn't want to think about the evil I had been surrounded with for the past eight years. Now, I only wanted to concentrate on the new family I'd been given thanks to falling for Max Reid.

EPILOGUE
MAX

Four Years Later

I lowered the car I'd just finished changing the oil in and then had one of the prospects who was interning at the garage drive it out of the bay. Walking into the shop, I gave my sister the slip for the customer.

"Unc!" Finn yelled from where he was playing behind the counter. "Is my new baby cousin born yet?"

Lexa, who had her five-month-old daughter, Tali, strapped to her chest in one of those wrap things, shot me an eye roll as she punched in the report on the computer in front of her. The beautiful little replica of my sister was sound asleep with the sound of her mother's heart as her lullaby. I doubted the baby girl would have even flinched if someone drove their car through the front window. She was a hard sleeper and being cradled against Lexa the way she currently was tended to be her favorite place in the universe.

For the past few months, Finn asked me that same question every time he saw me or his aunt Delaney. And each time, I had to disappoint him by telling him, "Not yet, bud. But soon."

At least, I hoped so. Delaney was a week past her due date and so miserable that she couldn't find a comfortable position, no matter what she did. Sitting up. Propped body pillows on either side of her. Being held by me. She was getting cranky because she couldn't sleep from the discomfort of our son putting pressure on her lower back and other places.

Thankfully, she was at Mom's today instead of working in the office doing all of our orders and the books. After she'd gotten her GED the summer we'd gotten married, she'd started taking business classes at Trinity and began working at the shop. I'd told her she didn't ever have to work if she didn't want to, but she hated sitting around doing nothing. She was stubborn and didn't want anyone to think she was with me only because of what I could give her.

No one had ever thought that, or if they had, they'd known better than to run their mouth. Not only would they have had me to deal with, but also Mom and Aunt Kelli as well. Plus, every other member of our family, River and Lexa both topping the list of those overly protective of my little treasure.

"I'm taking off," I informed my sister. "If you need anything, the prospect is shadowing Trigger for the rest of the day."

Lexa gave me a smile. "Give Delaney a kiss for me. Let me know if anything changes. I promised I would call Tavia as soon as there was activity suggesting Ronan is on his way."

"She should just wait and fly out at the end of the week

when they come to pick up Nova for the summer," I grumbled.

"You're just grumpy because you know everyone is going to be gushing over Delaney, and you won't get any cuddle time with your wife and newborn son."

I pressed my lips together, because she wasn't wrong. I knew the second Delaney went into labor, I would be lucky if I got to hold her hand with how all the women in my family had been acting lately. Mom and Kelli were already keeping me away from my treasure for most of the day as it was. When she went into labor, they were both supposed to be in the delivery room with us, and between the two of them, they took over my girl.

It wasn't that I didn't like that she was getting pampered by everyone. I loved that they were making her first pregnancy so special for her. But fuck if I didn't want a few hours alone to just hold my beautiful wife—and, when he arrived, Ronan too.

Picking up my keys, I gave Finn a fist bump before walking out the back door and climbing into the driver's seat of my SUV. For the last three months, I'd been mostly driving it around rather than my bike so I could take Delaney to and from wherever she needed to go each day. Mom, Kelli, and River were always trying to take her to her doctor's appointments or shopping for the baby's room in our new house just a block over from Lexa's place, but those three had gotten an earful from me. Didn't they trust me to do any of that stuff? And hey, I wanted to be at all of her prenatal appointments. I got a kick out of hearing Ronan's heartbeat at each visit.

Not to mention, I had to make sure the fucking doctor prick didn't linger when he was examining my wife's cervix or whatever the fuck he was doing when he was down there.

The guy was new to the area, had taken over for the local OB-GYN not long after River had her own baby boy, Rocco, and I needed to make sure he understood that Delaney Reid was only a patient and not someone he should even chance taking a second look at if he wanted to spend his life delivering more babies in Creswell Springs.

It wasn't like I was the only one to make sure the fucker understood that. Hell, Ben had been more than a little vocal when Lexa was pregnant with Tali. Not to mention Lyric when Mila had been pregnant with her second set of twins, Israel and Ireland. The doctor should have gotten the hint by the time Delaney became his patient, but no, the dickhead couldn't keep his eyes to himself when he had a beautiful woman on his exam table.

But I had to admit he was a really good doctor, and for that alone, I hadn't put a bullet in his skull.

Pulling up in front of Mom's house, I saw that Kelli's car was already in the driveway. It was nothing I didn't expect. If Delaney was at my parents' place, then so was Kelli. And if Delaney happened to be at Kelli's, Mom tended to be over there. It was like they were afraid to be too far away from her in case she went into labor and neither one of them was there.

And as much as I was aggravated that they were both hogging so much of the alone time I wanted with Delaney, I was still thankful they were taking such gentle care of her for me while I was at work.

Exiting the Tahoe, I walked up to the front porch, but before I could turn the knob, it opened. Nova grimaced as she glanced over her shoulder then back to me. "I'm going to warn you now—"

"Fuck," I muttered, already dreading what was going to come out of my cousin's mouth.

"She started having contractions about two hours ago. The lights are off and they have her comfortable, but she doesn't want to go to the hospital yet. Keeps saying she knows how grumpy you will be, and she wants things to be as calm for you as possible."

I raked my hands through my hair, my heart already thumping heavily against my chest at the thought of my treasure in pain. Of course, her only worry was for me.

"What should I do?" I asked Nova in desperation. "She should be at the hospital, but I don't want to stress her out."

She gave me a reassuring smile. "When you go in there, just sit with her. Aunt Raven and Aunt Kelli are taking turns rubbing her back and feet, trying to get her as comfortable as possible. My mom is feeding her ice chips, and the entire house is very zen right now." She patted me on the arm. "Take your cues from them, cuz. They are the ones with all the experience after all, seeing as they've each had a baby or two of their own."

I sucked in a deep breath, trying to steady myself. "You're right. Okay. I've got this." Tears stung my eyes for the first time since I could remember. "She's going to be okay, right?"

"Of course she is!" Nova gave me a quick hug. "Now, get your ass in there and hold your treasure's hand."

With that, she bounced down the stairs, her phone already to her ear. I could hear her speaking to Ryan, most likely letting him know that Ronan was on his way. I trusted that he would let Tavia know and figured they would be on their plane within the hour.

"Fuck," I muttered to myself again, but I opened the door and walked in.

As Nova had said, the house did have an instant zen vibe to it. The lights were off, and even though the AC was blasting, there was a fan pointed right at Delaney as she sat on the couch. Mom stood behind her, massaging her back, while Kelli sat on the coffee table in front of her, rubbing my very pregnant wife's swollen feet. Aunt Flick sat beside her, spooning crushed ice into Delaney's mouth.

Sweat dotted my treasure's upper lip and brow, making her face glow. Her cheeks were flushed, and when she opened her eyes as I walked closer, I could see they were glazed with pain. She gave me a bright smile as soon as she saw me. "Hi," she signed. "You're here early."

"I missed you," I told her honestly. "Thought I could come steal my beautiful wife for some cuddle time. Looks as if you need it."

"The contractions are only ten minutes apart," Kelli informed me, signing the words as she spoke them. She'd become fluent in ASL in the last four years, helping her become even closer to her niece. Between her and Mom, Delaney didn't feel the loss of not having her mom nearly as much as she used to. "They need to be closer together before we can go to the hospital."

I nodded, giving them all a tight smile, trying to hold it together for them—but more importantly, for my treasure.

Flick stood and handed me the container of crushed ice. As she did, she gave my arm a squeeze, whispering to me that everything was going to be fine and I could do this. I didn't know if she was right, but I schooled my face so my wife didn't see how freaked out and scared I was.

For the next three hours, I sat there, feeding her the ice and holding her hand. When she moaned in pain from the contractions, my heart rate would jack up a little higher, but I only rubbed her belly. It comforted her when I did, speaking to my son. I was just glad she couldn't hear the quiver in my voice when I told him how much I loved him, or she would know I was holding on by a thin thread.

Finally, the contractions were five minutes apart. By that time, Lexa and River had arrived, both of them having dropped their kids with their fathers. As soon as Mom said we could go to the hospital, I scooped up my treasure and sprinted to our Tahoe, making her giggle even as another hard contraction hit her.

That thin thread broke the second Delaney started pushing, not half an hour after we were placed in a labor and delivery room. She'd been adamant about no epidural, and there had been no time for one even if she'd changed her mind. Things had moved at warp speed, and the doctor barely had time to suit up before she was dilated to ten.

The first few pushes were fine. She did what Mom signed for her to do, exactly as we'd practiced. Ronan's head appeared, covered in thick, dark hair. But then the doctor said to wait before she pushed again, and she tried. The pain was too much for her, though, and she screamed when the doctor gave her the green light to push again.

My son's shoulders were wide, and she began to tear, causing her to scream again.

That was when I lost it. Her pain was too much for me, and I began sobbing, unable to control my emotions even for another second, let alone until she was no longer in excruciating pain.

With one more push, I watched as my son was born through my tears. Scrubbing a fist over my soaked face, I kissed my treasure.

Breathing hard from exertion, she widened her eyes when she saw the condition I was in. "Max?" she whispered.

"I'm okay, treasure," I rushed to assure her. "It was just hard to see you in pain." I kissed her again, swallowing down the next sob, but this one from total happiness. My wife had just given me the most amazing gift. "Our son is perfect."

Her concern morphed into an exhausted but content smile. "Just like you."

"No, treasure," I told her, and I watched the nurses clean off our firstborn. "Just like you."

FAMILY TREE: ROCKERS

Emmie & Nik: Mia (Barrick—Emerson and Hendrix), Jagger (Shaw)

Jesse & Layla: Lucy (Harris—Hayat and Evan), Luca (Violet—Remi, aka Love Bug), Lyric (Mila—Ian and Isaac, Israel and Ireland)

Drake & Lana: Nevaeh (Braxton—Conrad and Carver), Arella, Heavenleigh, Bliss, Damian

Shane & Harper: Violet (Luca—Remi, aka Love Bug), Mason

Axton & Dallas: Kenzie (Bishop—Knox and Vera), Cannon, Shaw (Jagger)

Wroth & Marissa: Jackson, Bryant, Liam, Dorothy/Doe

Devlin & Natalie: Harris (Lucy—Hayat and Evan), Trinity

Liam & Gabriella: Asher, Piper

Zander & Annabelle: Michelle, Mieke (Kaden—Michelle and Nash), Jaco

Linc & Rhett: Lennon, Ripley

Jenna & Angie: Iris, Morgana

Siblings

Drake, Shane, Natalie, Jenna

Layla, Lana, Lucy

Liam, Marissa

FAMILY TREE: MC

Raven & Bash: Lexa (Ben—Finn and Tali), Max (Delaney
—Ronan)

Spider & Willa: Maverick (River—Rocco), Mila (Lyric—
Isaac and Ian, Israel and Irland), Monroe (Gian—Gianna and
Lillianna)

Hawk & Gracie: Jack

Jet & Flick: Garret, Nova

Raider & Quinn: Kingston

Matt & Rory: Chance

Colt & Kelli: River (Maverick—Rocco)

Tanner & Jos: Reid, Elias

Siblings

Jet, Hawk, Raider, Colt, Raven

Tanner, Matt

FAMILY TREE: MAFIA

Scarlett & Ciro: Zayne, Zariah, Ciana, Vito, Benito

Victoria & Adrian: Theo (Tavia—Rai), Sofia

Allegra & Dante: Jenny, Adley, Mateo

Cristiano & Anya: Ryan, Samara

Siblings
    Cristiano, Scarlett, Victoria
    Adrian, Anya

MC/MAFIOSO KIDS BIRTH ORDER

Lexa—26
    Theo—25
    Reid—22
    Zayne—21
    Zariah—21
    Max—21
    Jack—19
    Kingston—19
    Maverick—19
    Mila—19
    Monroe—19
    Chance—19
    Elias—19
    Sofia—19
    Ryan—18
    Ciana—18
    Garret—18
    River—18
    Vito—14

Benito—14
Nova—13
Samara—8

TIMELINE READING ORDER FOR THE ROCKER…UNIVERSE

Our Broken Love Collection (Alexis)
    The Rocker Who Holds Me
    The Rocker Who Savors Me
    The Rocker Who Needs Me
    The Rocker Who Loves Me
    The Rocker Who Holds Her
    The Rockers' Babies
    Angel's Halo
    Angel's Halo Entangled
    Angel's Halo Guardian Angel
    The Rocker Who Wants Me
    The Rocker Who Cherishes Me
    The Rocker Who Shatters Me
    The Rocker Who Hates Me
    Angel's Halo Reclaimed
    The Rocker Who Betrays Me
    Defying Her Mafioso
    His Mafioso Princess
    Angel's Halo Atonement
    Angel's Halo Fallen Angel

Marrying Her Mafioso
Angel's Halo Avenged
Her Mafioso King
Angel's Halo Forever Angel
Forever Rockers
Needing Forever Vol 1
Catching Lucy
Craving Lucy
Rocking Kin
Un-Shattering Lucy
Needing the Memories
Tainted Kiss
Tainted Butterfly
Forever Lucy
Tainted Bastard
Tainted Heartbreak
Tainted Forever
Needing Forever Vol 2
Salvation
Holding Mia
Off-Limits
Needing Nevaeh
Sweet Agony
Savoring Mila
Surviving His Scars
Loving Violet
Wanting Shaw
Needing Arella
Sacred Vow
Her Shelter
Heartless Savage (Ryan & Nova)

PLAYLIST

"Chasing Cars" by Snow Patrol
"Everything" by Art of Dying
"Watch Over You" by Alter Bridge
"Beautiful Pain" by Andy Black
"ocean eyes" by Billie Eilish
"Middle Finger" by Bohnes
"Consequences" (orchestra) by Camila Cabello
"Every Breath You Take" by Chase Holfelder
"The Sound of Silence" by Disturbed
"Everything" by Lifehouse

www.ingramcontent.com/pod-product-compliance
Lightning Source LLC
Chambersburg PA
CBHW061518120726
48001CB00004B/1350